This book is to be returned on or before
the last date stamped below.

3235

Books by the same author

Friends and Foes Trilogy:
Pigeon Summer
No Friend of Mine
Room for a Stranger

A Long Way Home

HOUSE
OF
GHOSTS

ANN TURNBULL

WALKER BOOKS
AND SUBSIDIARIES
LONDON • BOSTON • SYDNEY

First published 2000 by Walker Books Ltd
87 Vauxhall Walk, London SE11 5HJ

This edition published 2001

2 4 6 8 10 9 7 5 3 1

Text © 2000 Ann Turnbull
Cover illustration © 2000 Paul Howard

The right of Ann Turnbull to be identified as author
of this work has been asserted by her in accordance with
the Copyright, Designs and Patents Act 1988

This book has been typeset in Sabon

Printed in Great Britain by
Cox & Wyman Ltd, Reading, Berkshire

British Library Cataloguing in Publication Data:
a catalogue record for this book is
available from the British Library

ISBN 0-7445-7883-3

*To the memory of my father,
with love and gratitude*

CHAPTER ONE

The removal van had gone. The house was full of packing cases and misplaced furniture. In a cat basket on the kitchen floor Charley scrabbled and miaowed. Grace thought: it's happened. We're here. She still felt, deep down, a knot of anxiety about the changes the move might bring, but here, now, was her new home – this old house with its secrets: crooked walls, uneven floors, and the shapes of blocked-up doorways visible under the wallpaper.

She dropped to her knees beside the basket and stroked Charley's paws with one finger through the wire mesh of the door.

"Can I let him out now?"

Mum and Mike were making tea.

Mike said, "Check the front door's shut first."

"It is." Grace undid the straps and opened the basket.

Charley emerged. He stalked around the kitchen, appalled. At intervals he emitted a long wailing distress call.

"Oh, Charley!" Mum sipped her tea. "I know how you feel. But it'll be all right. Honestly."

Grace scooped him up. He resisted her, legs rigid, head burrowing under her arm, but she held on. "I'll take him to see my room," she said.

She went upstairs. There were more packing cases on the landing, and a pile of Mum's paintings propped against the wall outside the room that was going to be the studio.

The room Grace had chosen for herself was at the back of the house, with a window overlooking the canal and the river. She went in. It looked different, lighter than when she had last seen it. Mum and Mike had stripped off the flowery wallpaper and painted the walls rose-white.

She shut the door so that Charley could not escape and then allowed him to vault out of her arms. He ranged the room, complaining.

Grace went to the window. The house was at the end of a terrace. It had a small garden enclosed by a brick wall with a gate on to the canal towpath, where ducks were sitting. Beyond the canal, at a lower level, was the river. She watched it sweeping past: a rough river, troubled with eddies and small whirlpools; fast, relentless. The supports of the nearby footbridge interrupted its movement, causing bubbles of white foam to break on the surface.

Charley was miaowing at the closed door. Grace left the window and went to stroke him. "Don't you like this room, Charley? We'll soon get it sorted."

Her bed and wardrobe were already in place, and there was a blue speckled carpet and faded curtains left by the previous owners. Two crates of books, games and soft toys (hoarded now, but no longer played with) stood in the middle of the room, next to a chest of drawers full of clothes. She needed shelves – Mike would put them up.

The only other place for her things was the triangular cupboard built into the corner of the room by the window: an old cupboard – Mike had said it was probably put there when the house was built, about 1830. It was divided horizontally into two sections, separated by a small drawer. Grace opened the two sets of doors and examined the spaces inside. The shelves in the top cupboard might do for games, she thought, those in the lower one for paper and felt pens and the piles of magazines she always kept.

"Not for cats," she said aloud. Charley had crept into the lower section and was sniffing about, his nostrils twitching. Wisps of cobweb clung to his whiskers.

Grace took a Scrabble set and some jigsaws

out of the crate and put them in the top cupboard. Charley sprang on to the second shelf of the lower section. He put his front feet up on something inside and squirmed forward, tail twitching.

Grace giggled. "Come out, Charley!" She grabbed hold of him, and he jumped down, dislodging a piece of wood which tumbled out on to the floor.

"Now you've broken something," she said, and picked it up.

It was heavy. And it was not part of the cupboard's construction, but a box: a narrow flat box about nine inches long with a hinged lid and a metal catch and a name carved into its top surface: *Wm. Ashley*.

She lifted the catch and opened the lid.

A paint box. Inset into the wood were seven china dishes containing cracked, discoloured paint. Alongside the paints lay two fine-tipped brushes, and in the lid were two china trays for mixing colours.

It looked very old.

Wm. Ashley. Wm. was William, she knew. But who was William Ashley – and where exactly had his paint box come from?

She squatted and looked from underneath into the lower section of the cupboard. The shape of the drawer above protruded into the space, but the drawer was only half the cupboard's width, and on either side of it was a small support beam. Grace felt around on top of the beams. There was space enough on either of those for the box. It must have been put there deliberately: hidden. And now her fingers encountered something else. Paper: a small tight roll, crumpled at one end where it had been forced against the cupboard wall. With mounting excitement she pulled it out.

There were two pieces of paper, rolled one inside the other. She laid them on the floor and smoothed them out, pushing away Charley, who was desperate to sit on them. One was a collection of little random pencil drawings: a primrose, a weeping willow, a bird on a branch, a rabbit by a tussock of grass. The primrose was quite good, but the bird and rabbit were badly proportioned. She wondered if William Ashley was a child. The other was a painting, very small and delicate, of a country scene with a river and a meadow sloping up from it, that rabbit again (slightly better drawn), and a red-roofed house in the distance, on a ridge.

The painting was signed, *Clemence Ashley, 1861*.

"Mum! Mike!" Grace picked up her finds and ran out on to the landing.

Mike was at the foot of the stairs, about to come up. "Oh, Grace! There you are. I'm going to Culverton to get a take-away – Indian. What do you want? Chicken Tikka?"

"Yes, please. Mike—"

"Naan?"

"Yes."

"Right. Won't be long!"

He was gone.

Mum was sorting things in the kitchen. Jars and packets of food and displaced familiar objects – the bread bin, the blender, the sugar tin – were herded together like refugees on the worktop.

"Mum, look what I found," said Grace.

Her mother glanced at the box and papers. "Not now, love. Show me later."

"Oh, Mum! Look! They were hidden in my cupboard."

Mum sighed, took the paint box, and opened it. At once her interest quickened. "This is wonderful, Grace! Look how the little trays fit in. And the colours are still there." She loosened the paint pots and took them out and ran water on to them, leaving them to soak in the washing-up bowl. She washed the brushes under the tap. "These are sable... You know, this wasn't a child's box; it belonged to an artist. I wonder if William Ashley was one of the painters from the china factory? The museum people might know. We could go along there tomorrow and ask them."

Grace reached out and retrieved the paint box while Mum was examining the pictures. The china museum was only just up the road, converted from the buildings that had once been the factory. She wondered if they would want to keep the things. But they're mine, she thought; I found them.

Mum said, "Clemence ... his son, perhaps? Or would that be a girl, do you think?"

Grace shrugged. "It's a weird name."

"A child, anyway. Too amateurish for the owner of those brushes."

"Are they good ones?" Grace stroked the fine tips.

"The best," said Mum. She smiled. "I like the idea of living where one of the old painters lived. It seems right."

She turned back to the kitchen clutter; but after a while she took one of the paint pots out of the water. The reddish-brown colour had begun to soften. "Here's burnt sienna," she said. "And this one looks like yellow ochre ... and cobalt..."

The two of them were still speculating about William Ashley when they heard the front door open, and Mike came in laden with spicy-smelling packages. "Right, I've got two tikkas, one vegetable biryani, rice, naans, onion bhajees, that banana spice thing—"

"Good grief!" said Mum.

"Oh, and poppadoms..." Mike enjoyed food.

Mum rushed to clear a space on the work-top and he began unloading all the boxes.

"I met that woman from the jewellery

workshop," he said, tipping rice on to a plate. "What's her name? Kathryn Cole? She was leaving as I arrived – a car-load of kids and a mad dog and about eight carrier bags of take-aways. She seemed friendly. Says she lives just across the bridge and will pop round."

Grace wondered whether the woman would bring her children and the mad dog. The thought was rather alarming.

"Mike," she said, "look at this..."

That night Grace put the paint box and papers on the chest of drawers next to her bed. Mike, who did a bit of antique dealing, was sure they were genuine and might well have been in the cupboard since 1861.

I was the first person to touch them since then, thought Grace.

For a while she lay awake, listening to the soft splashing of the river, feeling the strangeness of this new, quiet place. Then she fell asleep.

She was in the river. Water roared in her ears. She surfaced, gasped in panic, saw trees, branches, whipping past as the current swept her downstream. She was cold – so cold. Her long skirts were tangled around her legs and she kicked and fought to free them, but could not. The water submerged her, filling her mouth, and she spat, gasped, struck out for the shore. She saw trees standing above the flood, a branch she might reach. They wavered in her vision as she sank, rose again, and knew she was growing weaker. "Help! Help me!" She heard the words in her head but no sound came.

She woke up. The dream, dark and terrifying, clung about her, and she lay still for a moment with her eyes shut, hearing bird song, and letting the awareness of daylight slowly dissolve her fear. She opened her eyes.

Across the room stood a girl. Grace gasped, and sat up. The girl didn't move. She was about Grace's own age and was holding a little dog in her arms. She looked at Grace, and Grace looked back and saw her expression (scared, she thought – scared, and yet defiant). She took in the hair, plaited and looped on either side of the head, the old-fashioned, full-skirted dress – and then the girl was gone. There was just the wardrobe and the newly painted wall.

Grace began to shake.

I've seen a ghost, she thought.

CHAPTER TWO

"You imagined her," said Mike.

He tipped cornflakes into three bowls and opened a carton of milk. Mum, still in her nightdress, looked at Grace, concerned. "She saw *something*, Mike."

"She'd only just woken up – and from a bad dream. She was half asleep. The mind can play tricks..."

"It was real," insisted Grace. "She stood there, looking at me, with the dog in her arms. A real person. I'd know her again." She took a breath that shuddered. "I think she drowned."

"Oh, Grace!" They spoke together. Neither of them wanted to hear this.

"I dreamt of her in the river," said Grace. "I *was* her. I felt her long skirts tangling."

"Look –" Mike plonked a large bowl of cornflakes in front of her – "we make dreams out of the clutter in our minds – bits and pieces from our day. The river. The Victorian paint box. That's all it was."

Grace wanted to believe he was right. He was so confident, so down to earth. Maybe the dream *was* just a dream. But the girl – she'd been awake when she saw her. "I think the girl did the painting," she said. "I think she was Clemence Ashley."

"We'll go to the museum," Mum promised. She yawned. Seven-fifteen was early for her during half-term. "They might know something about the Ashleys. But first I must put up some curtains – at least in the bedrooms. I want a lie-in tomorrow."

Mike found the stepladder and they went off upstairs, arguing companionably about which curtains should go where. When they reached the landing their voices dropped, and Grace heard a worried note in Mum's voice and a reassuring one in Mike's, and she knew they were talking about her, discussing her state of mind.

She felt indignant. I shouldn't have told them, she thought. But she'd been so shocked, so excited, all her ideas about the world and how it was ordered thrown into sudden chaos.

From upstairs she heard Charley, wailing his way around the unfamiliar rooms. Mike shouted at him to shut up, and the miaowing came closer, down the stairs. Grace thought:

perhaps when he has wailed in every corner of the house he'll settle down. She found him, and enticed him on to her lap, but he was stiff, his body telling her of his distress at being moved.

"I didn't want to move, at first," she said, stroking him. It was only seven miles, but it was a change from town to country. And it meant that instead of walking to school on her own she'd have to go on the school bus; and Emma Fullerton and Zoe Bird went on that bus.

All the same, she liked this house better than the one in Brentbridge. Even with the ghost. Perhaps especially with the ghost – for now that the initial shock was over, she felt intensely curious, and almost hoped she might see it again.

Mum came downstairs, a swathe of green curtain over her arm. "Grace, why don't you start unpacking your stuff? Don't just flop about." She paused, then added anxiously, "Or are you... Do you want to change rooms? You can if you like."

"No," Grace said. "No, I like that room."

She left Charley and ran upstairs.

At the doorway she paused. But the room was ordinary, unhaunted. *Had* it just been a dream? She'd only know if it happened again. She sat on the bed, relaxed, half-closed her eyes...

Nothing.

Disappointed, she began unpacking one of the crates: books, Monopoly, Trivial Pursuit, bundles of *J17* and *Smash Hits*, felt-tip pens, notebooks, a see-through plastic pencil case...

She stopped, took out a pencil, and began to draw.

The face was no good – didn't look a bit like the girl. But she captured the hairstyle, with its centre parting and plaits looped up over the ears. She drew the dress: long sleeves, tight bodice buttoned to the neck, full skirt. The skirt stopped where the end of the bed had cut across her view. She sketched in the little dog – some sort of terrier. Behind the girl was – what? She struggled to remember. Not the wardrobe, which should have been there. She'd had a vague impression of some sort of wash-stand, of a large cream-coloured jug.

This must have been her room, she thought. Perhaps her bed was here, where mine is. Only the house can't have been quite the same, because Mike said ours is two houses knocked into one.

She went out on to the landing, where the doors to Mum's studio and bedroom stood open. It was hard to imagine a blank wall there. The Victorian house would have been much smaller and darker.

"Grace?" Mum was at the foot of the stairs. "Shall we go to the museum now?"

*   *   *

19

Everyone at the museum reacted just like Mum: "This is so exciting!" The curator, a woman named Liz Freeman, was called in. She told them, "William Ashley was one of the leading artists of the 1840s and 50s. We have some of his work here."

She led them into the museum (free of charge! thought Grace, impressed).

The first few rooms were full of flowery, gilded china of the sort you saw in stately homes. Grace had been to the museum before, but had not paid much attention to the china, being more interested in the reconstructions of kilns with their glowing furnaces. Now she looked carefully at the scenes painted on the plates and vases.

"They're so small and fine, these paintings," said Mum. "Look at the detail." Her own paintings were large airy water-colours.

Liz Freeman pointed out a teapot, pink with gilded garlands, and decorated with an oval painting of a country bridge over a river, with a village in the distance and flowers in the foreground. *Believed to be the work of William Ashley*, said the label.

"He specialized in landscapes and rural scenes," said Liz Freeman. "Here's another one that we think may be his."

"Don't you know?" Grace asked. Mum always signed and dated her paintings.

"No. The artists rarely signed their work.

20

They were just employees, you see. The individual wasn't so important then."

"And did he live in Upper Row? In our house?" asked Mum.

"I can check on that. One of my colleagues has been studying the census returns, looking for names and occupations. He's trying to build up a picture of the china workers' lives. I'll speak to him today." She smiled. "I must go. But thank you for coming in. The paint box –" she looked at Grace – "it's yours, of course. But it would be such an asset to the museum..."

Grace looked at her feet and did not reply.

When they left, Mum started laughing. "You were graceless, Grace!"

"I don't want her to have it. It's mine."

"Finders keepers?"

"Yes." But it had been good, finding out that William Ashley really was one of the artists. And perhaps soon she'd know about Clemence.

In the late afternoon Grace helped Mum carry some paintings across the footbridge to the craft centre where Mike had a gallery.

On the far side of the river two old warehouses had been converted into workshops. There was a potter, a toy-maker, a woman who made jewellery, a stained glass business. The cafe was closed; it would not open till

Easter. The sky was overcast, darkening already, and everything looked drab. There were no visitors, although a gang of children was running about and shouting at the far end, slamming the doors in the toilets and aggravating an already over-excited dog.

Mike's gallery was approached by an outside staircase and occupied the space above two of the workshops. Over the door a sign read, MICHAEL HOLBROOK – PICTURE FRAMING AND FINE ARTS. They went up.

The gallery was empty, except for Mike; they heard him whistling at the far end where the paintings were displayed. They walked between ranks of frames, mirrors, prints and posters.

Mike was rearranging paintings. There were two of Mum's there already. Mike had put her name up on the wall and there was a printed note about her at the side.

"Ah! Just in time!" Mike took the paintings from them and stood them against the wall, considering. "What do you think of the notice, Jane?" He grinned at Grace. "I'm raising your mother's profile."

"It's good," said Mum. "All we need now is some customers."

As she spoke the room darkened and a spatter of rain hit the window.

"They'll come," said Mike. "By Easter they'll be here. Always are."

Only they hardly ever buy anything, thought Grace.

Mike and Mum began sorting paintings. Grace left them to it and went out.

It was raining hard now and the craft centre looked less inviting than ever. She dashed for the entrance, where the children she had seen earlier were sheltering under the archway, their voices echoing in the stone space. One of them, a tall fair boy, looked vaguely familiar from school.

Grace felt them staring at her as she approached. She avoided their eyes and darted straight through and out on to the path.

Back home, she was aware of the house and all its rooms, empty around her. She'd never minded being on her own before, but now she was uneasy. She ran through the hall and downstairs rooms, switching on lights and calling, "Charley? Charley?"

He emerged from the living-room with a friendly chirrup and rose up, arching his back and lifting his front feet off the ground as she stroked him.

Grace put the radio on and fiddled around until she got Radio One.

The fridge made a cheerful humming sound. She opened it and found half a tin of cat food and emptied it into Charley's plate, talking to him all the time. She poured herself orange

23

juice and found some biscuits. Soon the house began to feel less threatening.

Charley was cleaning his whiskers. "Come on," Grace called to him. "Come up to my room."

He followed her out.

The hall was different. She noticed, briefly, that the lights seemed dim, that it was cold.

And then she stepped into a well of fear.

Her heart raced. There was a smell – a man's smell: sweat and hair oil, mixed with tobacco. And she glimpsed changes: dark brown walls; a long velvet curtain over the front door. A soundless roar was growing in her head, and out of it came a man's voice, hard, menacing: "Clem!"

She saw Charley, a pale blur, running upstairs. She fled after him, up to the landing, past the candle flickering on the window-sill. The voice came again, louder: "Clem!" He was close. The thought of seeing him filled her with terror.

With the cat at her feet she flung open the door of her room and fell inside.

CHAPTER THREE

It was dark.

She shut the door behind her and leaned against it. Her legs felt shaky.

If this is my time, she thought, the light switch will be on the wall to my left, about level with my eyes.

She reached up. Her fingers slid across the wall and found, to her intense relief, the familiar smooth plastic square.

She pressed the switch, flooding the room with light. She saw her bed, the blue carpet, the familiar clutter on the floor.

And she saw Charley.

He had a ridge of erect fur running from the nape of his neck to his tail, which was fluffed-up like a lavatory brush.

She dropped to her knees and stroked him. He felt electric.

"You heard it, too," she said.

She sat on the floor, cuddling Charley, until the ridge went down and he purred and kneaded her and her legs got pins and needles.

Then she thought about opening the door, and about what she might find outside, and didn't dare.

She got up, and paced around the room.

She felt shaken and confused, as well as frightened. Somehow she'd taken it for granted that they had loved each other: the child who kept the paint box and the father who painted those delicate water-colours. Yet surely it must have been the father's voice she'd heard: a strong, authoritative voice, of someone familiar enough to call the girl "Clem". Why was Clem afraid of him? What did he do? Did he drown her? Perhaps that was why her ghost was here.

Grace looked at the place across the room where she'd seen the ghost, and remembered how, only this morning, she had made her eyes go out of focus and willed herself to see it again. Not now, she thought. I'm scared. I don't want this.

From below she heard the sound of the front door opening; familiar voices; Mike's footsteps on the stairs. She felt a rush of relief.

She ran and opened the door and launched herself into his arms.

"Hey, steady on! Are you all right, pet?"

"Yes." Tears rose to her eyes. She buried her face in his jumper.

"What's the matter? Something scare you?"

She didn't know how to explain. If she said, "I heard a voice", he'd think she was going mad. "It's ... sort of quiet, here ... in the evening," she said.

That satisfied him – though he looked at her a bit anxiously, and she knew he was remembering the way she'd burst into their room that morning, crying that she'd seen a ghost.

"I'm all right," she assured him.

She longed to tell them both, but she knew they'd worry. Especially Mum. If she wasn't careful they'd be hauling her off to see the doctor.

The evening was ordinary, the house full of light and movement, no chance of seeing ghosts. They had dinner, and then Mum went upstairs to sort clothes while Mike and Grace watched *The X Files*. They always watched it together, and it was a relief to curl up on the settee and look at aliens and strange adventures, and forget about being haunted by an ordinary, unhappy girl. Afterwards she thought again of telling Mike about the voice, and that Charley had heard it too, but she didn't want to spoil the companionable atmosphere. And, besides, he'd probably find a way of rationalizing it: Charley picking up her fear, or something. It was strange, she thought, how Mike could sit there engrossed in *The X Files* and yet not believe in anything unusual happening in real life.

Later, when she said she was off to bed, she was aware of both of them watching her. She knew they were thinking about the ghost, but Mum only said, "You're happy with that room, then?"

"Yes. It's OK."

"You could have the spare room."

"It's OK."

"Don't fuss, Jane," said Mike.

"Well, leave the door ajar, if..."

"Jane!"

"I'll be all right," said Grace.

And she was. If she dreamt, she knew nothing of it, but woke late to the sound of the telephone ringing downstairs.

Mum answered it. Grace could tell from the way her voice changed that the caller wasn't family. "Oh! Really... That's fascinating... Yes, any time after nine-thirty... Ten would be fine..."

When Grace came down they both looked at her warily.

"I didn't dream," she said, and saw them relax. "Who was that on the phone?"

"Liz Freeman," said Mum. "From the museum. She's got some stuff to show us, about the Ashleys. She says there's a bit of a mystery about the date on the painting we showed her—"

"A mystery?" Grace began to feel excited, and a little apprehensive.

"But she's found Clemence Ashley."

"And was it a girl – his daughter?"

"I didn't ask. But Liz is coming round."

"At ten!"

"Ten tomorrow morning."

Grace was frantic with impatience. Tomorrow felt like a lifetime away. "Why can't she come now?"

"I don't know! She just said she'd pop in on her way to the museum tomorrow morning."

Mike infuriated Grace by laughing at her. "They're all dead, whoever they are. They can wait another day."

He went off to the gallery and Mum began organizing her studio. Grace, on Mum's orders, finished her unpacking. She hung up clothes in the wardrobe, stuffed things into drawers, sorted tapes and CDs. She found a rolled-up collection of posters, and asked Mum, "Can I put these up?" and Mum looked regretfully at the newly painted walls and said "yes". Several times Grace picked up Clemence Ashley's painting and looked at the date – 1861 – and wondered what the mystery could be. To take her mind off it she busied herself cutting out photographs from magazines and arranging them on the walls.

In the afternoon Mum got seriously involved in cleaning. The sound of the hoover drove Charley into the rainy garden and Grace over the bridge to the craft centre.

She bounced into the gallery and called, "Mike?" before she noticed that he had customers: an old man and woman, both in beige anoraks and carrying umbrellas that made dark trails of water on the floor. They were studying Mum's paintings and talking to Mike.

She began to back off, but Mike said in his charming-the-public voice, "And here's the girl herself – our daughter Grace."

"Oh!" The old woman turned and beamed at her. Grace realized they had been admiring *Home from School*, a painting of a girl flopped in an armchair with a school bag tossed on the floor, spilling books, and a large tabby cat on her lap.

She twisted about in embarrassment, avoiding the woman's smile. I'm not *our* daughter, she thought.

"Mike?" She hadn't come in to ask this, but now it seemed a good idea. "Can I get a Cornetto?"

"Haven't you got any money?"

"It's at home."

Mike fished in his pocket and gave her some change. "Go on – scat!"

As she came out she heard voices below. The children she had seen yesterday were clustered around the lowest steps: the fair-haired boy, a girl who was obviously his sister, and two much younger boys: a skinny six or seven year

30

old and a little one with a strident voice. A dog
– the over-excited Border collie she remembered – was racing around.

There was no way of ignoring them. They
had to move aside to let her through, and then
the dog greeted her like a long-lost friend,
leaping up and planting muddy paws on her
coat.

"Sasha! Get down!" The eldest boy pulled
the animal away. "Sorry."

"It's all right," said Grace. She knelt and
stroked the dog.

"I saw you yesterday," the boy said. "Is he
your dad? Michael Holbrook?"

"No. Stepfather."

"My mum –" he flicked a glance towards
the unit called KATHRYN COLE DESIGNS – "she
met him. Says you just moved here. You go to
Purley Manor, don't you? Are you in Year
Seven?"

Grace was small for a twelve-year-old. She
drew herself up. "Eight," she said. "I've got
Mrs Driver."

He pulled a face.

Grace grinned, encouraged. "We call her
Slave Driver."

"I'm in Year Ten," said Adam.

Grace felt shy. She stroked the dog again
and said, "I was going to get an ice cream."

The eyes of the two youngest boys fixed on
her with sudden interest.

"Adam, can we—"

"No."

"We could ask Mum."

"Go and ask then."

They darted away.

Adam moved off beside Grace. "I've got stuck with minding this lot for half-term."

The girl, who was about ten, retorted, "You're not minding me."

He ignored her. "What's your name?"

"Grace Evans."

She felt flattered and embarrassed by his attention. She didn't know any older boys – the boys in her class at school were just kids, and she scarcely noticed them. But some of the girls had boyfriends of Adam's age.

The two little ones ran up, panting. "She says we can!" shouted the youngest, and the other handed Adam a heap of change and added, "She said, 'Ice creams in February?'" and he rolled his eyes and staggered about, laughing.

Grace found herself part of a group heading for the newsagent's shop on the road outside the craft centre. All five of them poured in, engulfing the shop. Adam and his sister, Imogen, argued over what they could afford; the little ones hung over the edge of the freezer cabinet, grabbing and rejecting, bewildered by the choice.

When at last they were all outside, they

wandered back up the road, holding the ice creams in their cold hands. The littlest one, who looked about four, kept stooping down to allow the dog to lick his.

"It's freezing in that yard," Imogen complained. "Let's go home."

"Coming?" Adam asked Grace.

Grace felt uncertain, but he seemed to expect her to come, so she nodded. "OK."

There was a howl of anguish behind them. The little one had dropped his ice cream and the dog was eating it.

"Oh, Josh!" said Imogen.

Josh came up to her, hand outstretched, but she backed away. "You're not having mine."

"Ice cream!" wailed Josh. He was convulsed with tears.

"Here, have a lick of mine, then," said Adam. "And Luke, give him a lick of yours."

Grace felt obliged to offer hers, too. The sobs subsided.

Adam gobbled some of his fast and gave the rest to Josh, whose hand closed round it contentedly. "Now hold it tight."

Imogen, her own ice cream still intact, said to Grace, "Josh always drops things."

They had reached number three, Riverside. Outside, on the road, was a blue estate car with a Greenpeace sticker in the back. Sounds of classical music cascaded from the open downstairs windows.

"Dad's plastering," said Adam, as he opened the front door.

The dog rushed in, and a man's voice yelled, "Keep that animal out of my way!"

Adam grabbed the dog's collar. They went down a narrow hall and emerged into the most chaotic kitchen Grace had ever seen: the sink full of washing-up, a basket of damp clothes on a chair, packets of dog biscuits and corn-flakes apparently interchangeable on the table, jars and packets and trailing pot plants all around, Lego and more dog biscuits under-foot, a hamster cage in one corner.

Josh prodded the cage. "Wake up, Bilbo!" But Bilbo wisely stayed hidden.

The back door was open and it was from the extension being built to one side of it that the music issued. A man with a beard and dusty face and hands appeared. "Just keep Sasha and the kids out of my way, Adam. I thought you were all – oh, hello!"

"This is Grace," said Adam. "She lives over the bridge."

"Hello, Grace."

He had a booming voice. And all the chil-dren spoke at top volume, as if determined to be heard first. Grace thought she would never survive in such a family; no one would know she was there.

Imogen tugged at her arm. "Come and see my room."

They all bounded upstairs, and Imogen showed Grace a small room crammed with pony books and soft toys, with a crystal hanging in the window and a thing over the bed like a spider's web with feathers hanging from it that Imogen said was a dream-catcher. "It catches your bad dreams and lets the good ones through."

Grace wondered if a dream-catcher would filter out ghosts. She'd like one anyway, she thought; it was pretty.

Next door was the boys' room. Model dinosaurs hung from strings all over the ceiling and brushed against Grace's head as she went in. Josh was over-excited, leaping from bed to bed and roaring.

"He's being a Power Ranger," Luke explained. "He likes me to be the baddies but sometimes I get fed up."

The boys' bedroom had a tiny box-room leading off it and this was where Adam slept. Grace squeezed in beside him and stood in a few inches of floor space. Their arms were almost touching and she felt herself going hot with embarrassment. It was impossible to move away: she was surrounded by a computer, a television, stacked computer and music magazines, tapes, a shelf of books. A cardboard assemble-it-yourself skeleton and a black fur fabric spider dangled from the ceiling; school books were heaped on the floor. Every spare inch of wall was covered with pictures: film posters, a map of the stars, crop circles.

She tried to seem relaxed. "It's great," she said.

"It's all right when that lot shut up," said Adam, closing the door. He launched himself on to the bed and lay flat on his back. "I can reach nearly everything from here."

Grace moved, with relief, into the space he had vacated, and squatted down to look at the books: astronomy, *Unexplained Mysteries of the Ocean*, science fiction, Adrian Mole. "I've got that one," she said. "It's great. I like that old-age pensioner he visits."

He laughed. "And the dog – Sabre!"

"Yes! I love Sabre."

"When the extension's finished," said Adam, "I'm getting a new room. All mod cons: like, a wardrobe. Imagine!"

Grace thought of her own room, and the ghost. If only she could tell Adam about it. But he might laugh, and that would be unbearable.

"You're very tidy," she said, noticing the neat piles of clothes stored in cardboard boxes.

"Have to be." He sat up. "You wouldn't survive in here otherwise. You'd be buried under mounds of filthy clothes, rotting socks, old apple cores—"

She started to laugh.

There was a banging on the door.

"Go away!" shouted Adam.

"Adam!" called Imogen. The door opened and she burst in.

Adam bounced up on to his knees, his hands clenched. "What?" he demanded.

"Adam, will you and Grace come and play Cluedo? I'm trying to play it with Luke but Josh is being a pain—"

"No," said Adam.

"He keeps interfering." Imogen's voice had developed a whine.

Grace murmured, "I don't mind..." but Adam got up, pushed his sister out, and slammed the door.

"It won't last," he said.

And it didn't. Ten minutes later they were all playing Cluedo. Adam, resigned to the situation, was happily in charge, Imogen alternately elated and shouting, "It isn't fair!", Luke having trouble keeping his cards hidden and Josh being the police car. ("There isn't a police car," said Imogen. "There is now," said Adam.) Grace, quietly sifting cards and giving Luke some unobtrusive help, realized she was enjoying herself.

She stayed till six, then walked home across the bridge. It was dusk. The distant trees were a dark mass, and when she looked down river she saw shadowy areas under the overhanging branches. She remembered her dream, and hurried home.

CHAPTER FOUR

Mum had made two different spaghetti sauces for dinner: a bacon one for Mike and Grace, a mushroom one for herself.

"The Coles are vegetarians, too," said Grace. "Their mum grows sprouty things on the window-sill, in little trays."

"And what's she like?" asked Mum.

"She wasn't there. Just their dad. He's OK."

"What does he do?"

"I don't know." Why did adults always want to know things like that? "They lived in Wales before they came here. Adam can speak Welsh – a bit, anyway. He can swear in Welsh."

"Useful," said Mike.

They laughed.

"How old is Adam?" asked Mum.

"Fourteen. He's into astronomy and stuff and he knows about all those things like black holes and quasars. And he thinks UFOs could really be

38

alien spacecraft –" Mike was looking sceptical – "well, some of them, anyway, he says. He's read a lot about it, Mike. They've got a telescope, and he says when it's a clear night I can go round and have a look through it. And he says..."

She stopped, aware of Mike's amused expression.

"Well, he's obviously made a hit with you, this lad."

Grace knew she was blushing. "I just like him, that's all!" she said.

She jumped up from the table and put her empty plate in the sink.

Adam had asked her about Mike. "Do you get on with him?" And Grace's first thought had been yes, she did; Mike was the best thing that had happened to them since Dad left. But she couldn't say that; it wouldn't sound cool. "He aggravates me," she'd said. "Winds me up – you know?" Well, it's true, she thought.

She turned to go.

Mum called her back. "The dishwasher..."

Grace glowered at the messy pans on the worktop. "Oh, Mum!"

"Oh, Grace!"

That night, Grace lay in bed thinking about the ghost, and about Adam, and how she'd wanted to tell him. It was the biggest thing on her mind and she hadn't been able to say it. I'd need to know him better, she thought.

*   *   *

39

She woke to wind and rain and the sound of a dog howling close by. She got up and opened the curtains – and recoiled in shock. Last night there had been a lawn and a flower bed with the wintry remains of roses in it. Now she found herself looking down into a narrow yard, only half the width the garden had been. It was brick-paved, with a washing line and a shed with an open door. In the entrance to the shed sat a small dog – the same one she had last seen in the arms of Clem Ashley.

The dog ran out into the rain under the window and whimpered. It seemed to Grace that it could see her. She felt terrified. The dog could see her and yet it was dead – a ghost dog. It must be seeing Clem Ashley.

"I can't let you in," she said. "I daren't".

Had Clem said that too – long ago? The words seemed to have been waiting in the air.

The dog whined piteously.

"Go away, *please*," begged Grace. She snapped the curtains shut.

Instantly the whining stopped. She heard rain and bird song, and then the distant but unmistakeable sound of a car engine. When she dared to inch the curtains open again, there was the garden, with its lawn and flower bed.

She relaxed. But why had she seen the dog? Its gaze had been focused on her window – Clem's window. Had it been shut out in the yard as a punishment? To punish Clem? Had

William Ashley shut it out?

"Grace!" Mum called up the stairs. "Are you awake? Liz Freeman will be here soon."

The museum! Something about a mystery. Grace had forgotten. She hurried to get dressed.

Liz Freeman looked closely at the date on Clem's painting, which Grace had brought downstairs. "There's no doubt about it, is there? It's 1861. I thought perhaps we'd mistaken a five for a six, but—"

"That's definitely a six," said Mike.

Mum and Grace agreed. Grace felt impatient. Of course it was a six. 1861. What was this leading to?

"The thing is," said Liz, "the Ashley family were living in this house in 1851, but by 1861 they appear to have gone." She spread papers on the kitchen table. Charley, on Grace's lap, reached out a paw; Grace restrained him. "The census is taken every ten years. It records all the people actually present in the house on one particular night; so there might be a visitor, or a family member might be away from home. These are copies of some of the returns for this area in Victorian times. Here, you see, is your house in 1851 – number six, Upper Row."

Grace peered at the cramped writing, made grey and indistinct by the photocopier.

Liz interpreted. "Head of household:

William Ashley. Age: thirty-five. Occupation: china painter. That's clearly our man. With him live Ann, his wife, aged twenty-four, and Clemence, his daughter, aged three."

Grace did a simple calculation in her head. "So in 1861 that daughter – Clemence – would have been thirteen?"

She thought of the girl she had seen. "It's her," she said.

Mum knew what she meant. Grace caught the anxious glance. But Liz said, "Oh, yes. I'm sure it's her. Clemence was an unusual name at that time, just as it is now. But see what we have in 1861 – the year your picture was painted." She produced another photocopy. "Number six, Upper Row, is now occupied by John Ford, a clerk aged thirty-nine, and his wife – another Ann. No Ashleys. No daughter. And yet the painting could only have been put in the cupboard that year or later."

Grace felt a shiver go through her.

The daughter drowned, she thought. Clemence drowned.

But it didn't make sense. If Clemence died, she couldn't have painted the 1861 picture.

Mike suddenly laughed and thumped the table, causing Charley to leap off Grace's lap. "What was the exact date of the 1861 census?" he asked.

"Seventh of April," said Liz Freeman. "Ah, I see what you mean—"

"This daughter did the painting early in that year, before the seventh of April, and put the stuff in the cupboard, and then the family moved..."

"Yes. Of course." The grown-ups were satisfied.

Grace asked the obvious question. "But why did she leave it behind?"

Mike shrugged. "Forgot it?"

You wouldn't forget something you'd only just hidden, thought Grace. Unless you'd died.

"Could we keep the photocopies?" Mum asked. "It's interesting to know who used to live around here."

"Yes, of course. And if you find anything else..."

Grace busied herself stroking Charley. The paint box was in its old hiding place upstairs, safe from the museum.

Back in her room, with Clem's papers on the bed in front of her, Grace thought about what she knew: Clem had painted her picture in 1861, sometime between January and the beginning of April; she was afraid of her father; she loved her little dog but someone had shut it out in the yard.

And she drowned.

Grace couldn't be sure of that; it was only a dream, and yet she felt sure that the dream and the ghost were connected.

She got up and went to the window. Beyond the garden and canal, the river was high: a broad tannin-coloured flood, flying past at extraordinary speed, like traffic on a motorway, bubbles of foam flecking its surface. There were drowned trees and bushes at its margin.

She remembered, in her dream, seeing the half-submerged branches, struggling to reach them. The river had been in flood when Clem died, early in 1861; as it was now.

Grace felt as if she was on the brink of discovering some terrible secret that she didn't want to know, and she was filled with foreboding. Whatever happened, she thought, it's all going to happen again. And I won't be able to stop it.

A figure came into view, walking along the canal towpath: Adam. The collie was frisking around him. Grace watched to see whether Imogen or the little ones would appear; to her relief he seemed to be alone. He glanced up briefly as he came level with the house, and she drew back from the window, suddenly self-conscious.

But she wanted to meet him. She ran downstairs and grabbed her coat and trainers.

"I'm going out."

"Mind the river," said her mother – as if I might otherwise trip over it, thought Grace. At Brentbridge it had always been "Mind the road".

She went out of the back gate, on to the canal path, hoping that she could pretend to have met him accidentally; but he was some way off, near the museum, and had his back to her.

She was too shy to call or run after him. She'd have run after a girl, perhaps; but it was different with a boy. A boy might think you fancied him.

She turned away, and climbed the steps that led first to the path that Mike said was once a railway line, and then up the steep wooded side of the gorge. A fuzz of pale green softened the bare trees, and she saw buds and catkins. She reached the top and came out in a meadow.

And there was Clem Ashley.

Grace saw her striding ahead across the tussocky grass, a fringed shawl around her shoulders, the little terrier running beside her. Her boots were muddy, and the hem of her brown skirt had clumps of mud clinging to it. She was swinging her arm back to throw a stick for the dog. Grace watched the stick fly, and as she turned she realized that the landscape had changed: she had an impression of fewer trees, more buildings, a railway line, a smoking chimney; and, on the river by the china museum, a thicket of masts and furled brown sails.

She put her hands over her face. It was all

45

around her. All haunted. She turned back to Clem, opening her eyes – but the girl had gone, and there was only the quiet meadow and, when she looked again, the deep tree-filled side of the gorge overlooking the empty river.

Leave me alone, she thought.

She scrambled back down the steps to the canal-side road. In the distance she saw Adam walking towards her. This time she ran to meet him.

CHAPTER FIVE

"Come down here," said Adam. He led the way on to the riverside path. She followed him, still shocked from her encounter with the ghost.

The water was high up the bank, sucking twigs and small branches into its swift brown current.

"I reckon it'll flood," said Adam, with satisfaction. "Our house gets cut off from the bridge sometimes."

"I saw the flood level mark on the end house." She felt jealous. There was no chance of Upper Row being flooded. She wondered if the Coles would be unable to get to school.

"No such luck," said Adam. "We can go out the back way – and the bus always gets through."

The bus. She'd be going on it tomorrow. She watched a twig caught and turning in one of the tiny whirlpools in the current. "I've never been on that bus before," she said.

Adam was not reassuring. "There's this stupid lot that keep chucking stuff around and fighting. I mean, you don't mind messing around a bit, do you? But they're just mad."

"Two girls in my class go on it," said Grace. "Emma Fullerton and Zoe Bird. I can't stand them."

She meant "I'm afraid of them." They never left her alone, and it would be awful, she realized, if they saw her get on the bus with Adam.

"I don't know any of the girls," said Adam dismissively.

They walked on, past the museum, under the road bridge, following the muddy riverside path. Sasha kept running ahead and back again. Sometimes the path rose high above a tangle of roots or a small cliff; sometimes it dipped low and ran almost on a level with the spreading flood.

They came to a bend in the river. A middle-aged couple with a dog had paused there to look at the view. On the far side of the river were fields, but on this side the woodland stretched to the water's edge, making the path increasingly difficult to follow. Adam led Grace out on to what looked like a sandbank that jutted into the river. But it wasn't sand; it felt brittle and clinked as she walked on it.

"It's all china!" she said.

The bank was made up of thousands of pieces of broken china and tile. They began picking them up, commenting on the names and patterns.

Grace felt at ease, contented. She liked doing this. She enjoyed Adam's company; with him she didn't have to pretend to be a different kind of person, the way she often did with the girls at school.

The couple were watching them. The man smiled. "Everything fetches up on that bank," he said. "Two hundred years or more that's been growing."

"Has it?" Adam began picking over the shards. "These could be really old, then! Why do they pile up here?"

"It's the current, that's why. The whirlpool. See how the water swirls just here? They reach the pool and can't get out. Broken china, rubbish, bodies... All the drownings end up here. And there's been a few drownings, over the years. Round and round they go, in the pool. That's where they're hauled out, most of them."

Grace stared at the pool, imagining Clem, the struggle over, going round and round. "Don't any get swept away?"

"Oh, yes – a few. If they can get through that narrow channel over there they'll go fast, no stopping them, could be all the way to Bristol. Some bodies are never found."

The woman laughed. "You and your stories!" She turned to Adam. "I wouldn't bother going much further. The path's flooded up ahead."

"Right. Thanks."

"Mind how you go."

They moved off. Adam and Grace went a little further along the path before being defeated by the tangle of overgrown branches and the encroaching flood.

"Home," said Adam. "Back to the mob." He pulled a face. "Luke and Josh were manic this morning."

Grace smiled. He likes them really, she thought. She wondered how she would feel about little brothers and sisters. And, not for the first time, she wondered if her mother would have a baby now that she was married to Mike. Adam picked up a stick and threw it, and Sasha raced away, her ears flying back. She returned and waited, quivering, for him to throw it again.

This time the throw went wide, and the stick fell into the water. Grace felt sudden panic as Sasha plunged into the river and struck out for the stick. "No!" she exclaimed. A name came into her head and she called after the dog: "Brush! Brush!"

She ran, and Adam ran after her.

"It's all right," he said. "She's OK."

He was staring at her, and Grace, her fear gone, felt herself going pink as she tried to remember what she had said.

This is Clem again, she thought.

The dog came out of the river, streaming wet.

Adam said, "Oh, no!" and moved away – too late. Sasha shook herself, and a fine speckling of muddy droplets covered both of them from waist to ankle. With shouts of laughter they scrambled up the bank.

Grace patted the dog. She thought the interruption would have made Adam forget. But it hadn't.

"Her name's Sasha," he said.

"I know." Grace hid her face in the dog's fur.

"You called her Brush."

"No, I didn't." She'd only just met Adam, and now he'd think she was stupid.

"You looked weird just then," said Adam.

"Thanks!" But her chin trembled, and it didn't sound like a joke. Adam looked surprised, and concerned. I'll have to explain, she thought.

She said, "Do you believe in ghosts?"

His face took on, at first, the sceptical look she'd got used to seeing on Mike's; but there was interest there too.

"I'm not kidding," she said. "I'm being haunted."

"My mum believes in ghosts," said Adam. He spoke cautiously, and she knew he still wasn't sure whether this was some sort of game. "Well, not ghosts exactly: past lives and stuff."

Grace didn't know anything about past lives. "It's a ghost," she insisted. "A girl that used to live in our house. I keep seeing her."

"And she had a dog called Brush?"

"I suppose so. I didn't know its name until I said it. I hear it barking..." She paused, thinking about this. "Sometimes I see things, and it's silent, like a silent film; but other times I hear them, or have a strange feeling. Like just now... The thing is, it's happening more and more. It's sort of building up to something. And the river's in flood. And I think she drowned."

His eyes widened. She had his interest now, and she felt a flicker of triumph mixed with the embarrassment and the desperate need to tell someone about it. She told him everything: about finding the paint box and pictures, the dream, the sightings, what the museum people had found out and what she'd guessed herself.

When she finished Adam said, "Weird!"

Grace searched his expression for support. "You do believe me?"

"Yes, of course." He seemed sincere. "Can we go to your house? See if it happens to me?"

It won't, she thought. But she wanted him to come with her.

They went through the canal gate into the back garden. Adam tied Sasha to the washing-line post.

In the kitchen Grace found a note from Mum: *Gone to gallery*. She felt relieved; she'd have been shyer with Mum around.

"Orange juice?" she asked Adam.

"Yes, please."

She opened the fridge, and at once Charley appeared and hovered by his bowl, miaowing. Grace gave him milk. They watched his small pink tongue darting in and out – "So tidy," said Adam. "Not like Sasha. She slobbers." He gave a demonstration; Grace giggled, and Charley paused in his lapping and fixed them both with an offended stare.

"Sorry, cat!" said Adam. He looked around the room. "So where did you see this ghost?"

"Not in here. In the hall, once; that's where I heard that voice..."

It was hard to believe, now. The hall was bright; a vase of daffodils stood on the tele-phone table.

"Come up to my room." Grace called Charley and led the way.

Adam looked around at the book shelves, the corner cupboard, the posters on the walls. "It's a good size." He went to the window. Sasha saw him and began to bark. "Is this where the garden changed?"

"Yes." She explained what she'd seen. "And

I saw the girl, just there, where the wardrobe is."

He stared at the place.

"She won't come now," said Grace. "She comes when you're not expecting her."

But Adam wanted to try.

They sat on the bed, facing the wardrobe. Charley leapt up, tested Adam's lap with a cautious paw, then played safe and went to Grace. Silence settled around them. Adam stared at the wall as if in a trance.

When at last he looked away, Grace said, "It won't work. I told you."

"You could be making all this up."

He's protecting himself, she thought, so that if I turn round in the end and say it was a joke he can pretend he knew all along.

"I think it's just me," she said. "Mum and Mike don't see her."

Adam reached out and stroked Charley, who changed allegiance and decamped to his lap. "I watched this programme on TV once, about poltergeists. There always seemed to be a young girl involved – a nutty girl..." He was grinning.

"Shut up, you!" She laughed, but felt an underlying anxiety. Was that how he saw her?

She jumped up. "I'll show you the things I found. They're hers."

The paint box impressed him. "It's great. We've never found anything interesting in our house."

"This used to be two houses. Half the rooms are really next door. But Clemence Ashley lived in this half."

"It would be different, then, when you see the ghost ... different walls and rooms?"

She nodded, trying to remember. "It's hard to work out what's changed."

"I wish I could see her!"

"You wouldn't." She tried to explain, but it was impossible to convey to someone who hadn't experienced it that this wasn't an intriguing game; it was real. "It's horrible," she said. "Something horrible happened to Clem."

Outside, in the garden, a dog was barking. Sasha. Surely it was Sasha? Suddenly uncertain, she went to the window. Sasha looked up, wagging her tail.

"I'd better take her home," said Adam.

When Adam had gone, Grace thought about his visit and felt glad she had told him. Even if he didn't quite understand how frightening it was, he'd assured her, as he left, that he did believe her, and he'd said he would think about how they could find out what happened – which must mean he wanted to see her again.

Mum came home and shut herself into her studio. Grace spent the afternoon doing homework. At four o'clock, bored and thirsty, she went down to the kitchen; on her way back she saw the photocopied census returns lying on the dresser. She took them upstairs and lay on her bed looking at them.

A large family named Willetts had lived next door at number five, she noticed. Daughters Ann, Mary and Elizabeth. Sons John and Robert. She imagined them all shouting and arguing like the Coles. How did they fit into that tiny house? For it must have been tiny, if it was only half of this house.

Funny, Grace thought: Mum's in her studio in number five, and I'm just across the landing in number six – where something happened to the Ashley family in 1861.

She looked again at the returns for number six, feeling almost resentful of those Fords, mysteriously appearing where Ashleys should have been.

John Ford. Age thirty-nine years.

Ann Ford. Wife. Age thirty-four years.

Ann.

Wasn't William Ashley's wife Ann?

She checked again: *Ann Ashley. Wife. Age twenty-four years.*

Twenty-four in 1851; thirty-four in 1861.

It was the same Ann. It had to be.

William Ashley must have died. He died, and Clemence, his daughter, kept his paint box and brushes. And her mother re-married.

She jumped up and ran and knocked on the studio door. "Mum?"

Mum wore old jeans and had her hair tied back with a ribbon. She was sorting frames.

Grace explained. "Look. It's the same person."

Her mother studied the two returns. "It could be," she said, "but it's just as likely to be a coincidence. Ann is a very common name. And where's the daughter?"

There was a silence between them. Mum knew what it meant. "You're not still worrying about that dream, are you?"

"Well, it's strange, isn't it? The way it fits."

"It is strange," Mum admitted.

But when Mike came home, he was dismissive. "Of course it fits. She's making it fit. Suppose she's right and it is the same woman? The census is a record of one night, right? Perhaps the daughter was away that night. Perhaps she was in hospital. Perhaps she was visiting her granny." He turned to Grace. "More to the point: it's school tomorrow. Have you done your homework?"

"Nearly." She felt irritated by the change of subject.

"Nearly! For heaven's sake, Grace, you've had all week!"

"I'll finish it after dinner." You're not my dad, she thought; you can't tell me what to do.

But now they were both on at her.

"You'd better clean your shoes," said Mum.

57

"And get your things ready: your PE clothes, your dinner money..."

Grace sighed theatrically. "I will."

It was eight o'clock before she got back to her homework. It was Geography. Boring. She scrawled rapidly, making her writing as wide as possible, then slapped the book shut and tossed it into her bag.

She lay on the bed, thinking about tomorrow: Adam, and the bus, and Emma Fullerton and Zoe Bird. Those girls didn't know she'd moved, wouldn't be expecting to see her. They'd latch on to her straight away. And Adam would witness her humiliation.

If only I didn't have to go, she thought. But it was close now; there was no escape.

Outside, rain beat on the window. She imagined the river rising relentlessly, carrying torn trees, china debris, boats, bodies...

A thought came to her. She reached for the census returns and looked again at the dates, realizing, with rising excitement, the significance of her earlier discovery.

The voice she'd heard in the hall wasn't William Ashley's. It wasn't her father Clem was afraid of. Grace felt a sense of rightness, of things falling into place. The gift of the paint box, the picture painted in her father's style, were evidence of affection. Clem had loved her father. The man she feared was her stepfather, John Ford.

CHAPTER SIX

They started as soon as she climbed aboard the bus: "Oh, how *amazing*! It's Grace!" That was Zoe Bird. Laughter spread around amongst the rest of the Culverton crowd. Then came the nasal singing: "Der der, der der der der..."

She glimpsed Adam making for the back through a seething mass of boys. Thank goodness he had ignored her as they climbed aboard; she hoped the Culverton girls hadn't seen them talking at the bus stop.

The bus throbbed with noise: thirty-odd voices competing. She looked round quickly for a seat – a place to slide in and be anonymous. There was one two rows in front of Emma Fullerton, next to a small thin girl who was chewing gum. She sat down quickly.

Brentbridge was only a quarter of an hour away by car, but the bus moved off ponderously along the winding lane, and stopped in the next village to let more people on; the journey would take forty minutes, she knew.

The girl next to her began doodling with a biro on the back of her left hand. Zoe Bird was having a shouted conversation with a boy. There were sounds of scuffles further back but Grace didn't want to turn round and see what was happening for fear of making eye contact with Emma.

A ball of paper hit her on the side of the head. "Hey!" Snorts of laughter. "Great Heavens! I mean Grace Evans!"

She ignored them.

"Have you moved house, Grace Heavens?"

"She's too stuck-up to tell us."

"Oh, please tell us, Your Grace."

Grace kept her head down. She was acutely aware of the presence of Adam at the back of the bus. Had he noticed? If he had, he'd know now that she was not worth bothering with.

A scrum of boys erupted down the aisle and distracted her tormentors. Zoe squealed. Emma began shouting something cheerfully obscene at a boy on the back seat. He replied in similar terms.

The bus had stopped at Chiddington. The driver turned round. "I'm not moving this bus till you all sit down. And mind your language."

They fought and swore a bit longer, then subsided.

Grace saw the driver's eyes reflected in his

mirror; he looked resigned.

The bus manoeuvred its way around the village green and on to the next stop.

Grace heard Emma and Zoe baiting her again. She stared out of the window, pretending not to notice. At last the outskirts of Brentbridge appeared, then Purley Manor School. The girl next to her removed the chewing gum from her mouth and pressed it on to the window pane.

The Culverton gang pushed their way down the aisle first, still shouting. Emma Fullerton hefted her school bag on to her shoulder, hitting Grace on the head. "Oh! Sorry, your Grace!"

Grace squeezed out, just in front of a surge of boys, whose jostling elbows caught her in the back. Climbing down, she watched them move away towards the plate glass and concrete building. Adam was amongst them – not rowdy, not being bullied: just part of the crowd. How did he do it? What did you have to do, not to be picked on? She couldn't see him doing anything in particular.

She attached herself to a group going into her class: Sara, Lauren and Naomi. If anyone had asked her who her mates were, she would have named those three, who were always friendly enough – though she never felt truly part of the group.

"I came on the bus today," she told Naomi.

"Were that Culverton lot on it?"

"Yes. You know, Emma Full-of-Herself—"

"And Zoe Turd."

They fell towards each other, giggling, and Grace felt better.

"If you didn't bring your money for the china museum trip before half-term, please remember to do so by Thursday," said Mrs Driver.

Grace had forgotten about the trip, although she had paid. It had been arranged at the end of last term, before she knew they were moving to Hazeley. It would seem funny going on a trip to a place so close to home; she wondered whether she'd need to go in to school that day.

They were studying Victorian industries, a subject which Grace, until last week, had found boring. Not any more. She began thinking again about what she had discovered yesterday. She felt sure she was right: that John Ford was Clem's step-father and that he was the one she was afraid of. But why? What did he do? And what happened to Clem?

Naomi nudged her. "Homework!" she whispered. "Give it in."

Grace came back to the present and rummaged in her bag.

The bus was worse on the way back. Emma Fullerton was in priestly mode. "Let us say grace," she intoned; and the mob roared, "GRACE!" – the name reverberating up and down the aisle. Grace felt frightened and humiliated. She wanted to die. What must Adam think of her now? There was no hope that he would not realize what was happening to her. But when they got off the bus – just the two of them at Hazeley – all he said was, "That Emma's a loud-mouthed cow, isn't she?" Grace felt enormously relieved.

It was almost dusk, the evening closing in early under low clouds.

"I've been thinking," said Adam, "about your ghost. If she drowned..."

Grace looked at the river, a yellow-brown flood, tugging, capturing everything in its path. She remembered her dream. "I'm sure she did."

"Then we might be able to find her grave," said Adam.

"Yes!" She felt exhilarated, both at the thought that they might find Clem, and at the prospect of searching for her with Adam. She turned to him eagerly. "There's an old church near your house, isn't there?"

"St Leonard's," said Adam. "We could go now. Have a look."

The graveyard of St Leonard's Church was full, but not large. If she's here, Grace thought, we should find her. She felt almost reluctant, now, to look and confirm that the girl she'd seen had died at the age of thirteen. But that's silly, she thought; she's dead anyway.

They ignored the shiny modern tombstones

and went further in, under dark evergreens, where the paths were padded with pine needles, and began their search amongst the old lichen-spotted, leaning stones. Many of these were not old enough. 1880, 1897 ... the ones that dated back as far as 1860 were worn and blackened. "Like the church," said Adam. "My dad says it's pollution – all those factories they had round here."

There were a few big tombs that looked like Ancient Egyptian sarcophagi; they had railings round them, and names and verses on all sides. "Too posh," Grace said, thinking of Clem in her muddy boots.

They split up and walked along separate paths. Grace read to herself a roll-call of faded names: so many Marys, Elizabeths and Sarahs. But no Clemence.

Then Adam called, "Grace! Here!"

She ran, conscious of her heartbeat, wanting and yet not wanting to know.

"She's not here," Adam said quickly. "But look."

The grave was under a tree, and the roots had tilted it backwards. It was stained with yellow blotches of lichen that obliterated some of the words:

SACRED TO THE MEMORY ...
WILL...M ASHLEY,
DIED 15 JU... 1859, AGED 43 YEARS.

Clem's father, William Ashley. So she had been right. William Ashley had died two years before the census was taken – before whatever happened to Clem.

"I found something else, too," said Adam.

Next to William Ashley's grave was another stone with three names on it:

THOMAS ASHLEY ... 12 JULY 1854
AGED THREE MONTHS.

MARY ASHLEY, DIED 3 JAN... 1857
... FIVE YEARS.

ISAAC ASHLEY ... 1858
... TWO YEARS.

DEARLY LOVED CHIL...
OF WILLIAM ...D ANN ASHLEY.

So they'd had other children. Grace knelt and pushed down the turf at the foot of the stone, but there was nothing else – no Clemence.

"That's sad," she said. "They were so young."

Adam squatted beside her. "I've looked all around, but I can't find Clemence."

The back of the graveyard was a thicket of thorn and bramble. There were gravestones sunk low in the earth, their wording almost gone. They struggled in amongst them, only half serious now, knowing they wouldn't find her. The search became a lark. Adam got caught on a trailing strand of bramble and Grace went to free him, catching her hand on the thorns. A bright line of blood sprang up.

She sucked her hand.

"Sorry," said Adam. They smiled.

"She's not here."

"No."

And it was getting dark. They picked up their school bags. With a mixture of disappointment and relief Grace followed him out and let the iron gate fall shut behind her.

"You're a bit late," Mum said.

"I was … talking to Adam." She regretted the words as soon as she'd said them.

"Oh!" Mum smiled.

It's not "Oh!" thought Grace. Or was it? Was that why she was embarrassed? She admitted to herself that she'd enjoyed scrambling around with Adam in the churchyard. But he's not my boyfriend, she thought; I don't want a boyfriend – not yet.

"We were just looking at graves," she said. "And guess what? We found William Ashley. He *did* die before 1861. So I was right."

Mum appeared taken aback – almost shocked. She said, "They could still have moved away – his widow and daughter. It might not be the same Ann." But she didn't sound as if she believed it, and she looked at

66

Grace searchingly. "You haven't been seeing … anything?"

Grace felt that it would be wise to lie. "No."

"Good." She changed the subject. "And how was the bus?"

Grace shrugged, and looked away. "OK."

"You do like living here, don't you?"

What was up with her? "It's OK."

Grace went to the fridge and poured herself some orange juice. "Can I have a biscuit?"

Mum discouraged biscuit eating. She thought you should have things like dried apricots. But now she said, "Yes. Go on." She added, "It'll get better – the bus." And stood biting her lower lip.

Grace took a second biscuit, picked up her bag, and went into the hall.

She heard the voices first. They seemed to come from nowhere in particular – in her head, or in the air around her. The girl's voice, high: "Leave me alone! Don't! Don't! Ma, don't let him hurt me!" The man's, grunting with exertion: "You will learn to obey!" Then bangs, sounds of struggle, footsteps. And the girl again, screaming.

Grace froze. The hall had darkened. She saw the velvet door-curtain, the strip of carpet up the centre of the stairs.

There was no way out. Should she run upstairs, or back to the kitchen? She turned, and saw in the kitchen doorway, the figure of a woman – a woman in a long Victorian dress, the bodice let out to accommodate her advanced pregnancy. She was flinching, her face screwed up, and she stood with a fist to her mouth, biting her thumbnail, while from overhead came the sound of the leather strap and the rising screams.

Help her! thought Grace. Help her!

But the woman was gone, and the sounds were gone, and Grace turned round and saw the white-painted hall with the vase of daffodils and the mirror, and her own shocked reflection.

She trembled as she climbed the stairs. The landing was safe, but there was a feeling, a prickle in the air, as if something had just happened, or was waiting just out of sight. The feeling was in her room, too.

She dropped her school bag and sat down on the bed. She could not stop shaking. She was not used to violence. No adult had ever hit her. And Clem was so helpless; her mother couldn't, or wouldn't, intervene.

"Clem." She spoke the name aloud into the charged air. "Why am I seeing all this? What do you want me to do?"

There was no response, yet she felt sure that Clem was there.

CHAPTER SEVEN

She woke thinking of the dog, Brush. She'd heard him in her dream, whimpering, his claws scrabbling at the wood of the back door below her window. But now there was no sound, not even birdsong; the silence felt loud.

She opened her eyes and saw Clem. The girl was standing, partially silhouetted against the light from the window, looking out. She wore a short-sleeved petticoat, and Grace was shocked by the black bruises on her upper arms. Clem seized the sash window and pushed it up without sound. The curtains blew inwards and Grace was near enough to see goose pimples appear on Clem's arm, but she could not feel the breeze.

The girl leaned out, wiping her eyes with the flat of her hand.

She wants the dog up here with her, Grace thought; and her sympathy with Clem was so strong that she imagined she could see a dent on the bedclothes where he ought to be, and remember the rough, springy feel of his fur. Perhaps before Clem's father died Brush had always lived indoors and slept on her bed. But now someone had parted them.

Clem's figure disappeared. The shell of silence broke and Grace heard birds, traffic, gurgling pipes in the bathroom, the creak of floorboards. She saw that the window was closed, the curtains drawn.

And yet the room still felt haunted.

She looked at her bedside clock. It was time to get up.

Cautiously she slid out of bed, opened the door, and ventured on to the landing.

Nothing. Nothing visible; and yet she sensed an undertone of fear, of things unseen, that made the hairs rise on the back of her neck.

The bathroom was a haven: ordinary, without atmosphere. She washed, and came out, and felt again the charged air of the landing. She padded across to the spare room; it was there too, though weaker.

Mum and Mike were downstairs; she could hear their voices. She crossed the width of the landing to their room, and felt a difference. The fear was gone. Their bedroom was like a pool of clear water, untainted. The difference was so great that she knew she was not imagining it. The feeling came back as soon as she crossed the landing, and it stayed with her while she got dressed and went down the stairs and through the hall, only dissipating as she approached the open door of the kitchen.

And suddenly she understood. It was number six that was haunted – the house where Clem had lived. But two houses had been knocked into one, and rooms changed around. Mum's studio and bedroom were in what had been number five; that was why she had felt a change as she crossed the landing.

Mum and Mike were having breakfast and talking about a painting. Grace realized one of Mum's had been sold – a rare event, unless she had an exhibition.

"*Home from School*," Mike said. "I sold it yesterday."

"Hey, that's a big one!" Grace was impressed. Big paintings cost more. It was funny to think of a painting of herself and Charley hanging in someone else's house: her own school bag, her own rumpled socks, the familiar wicker chair and patchwork cushion – a little bit of her life living somewhere else.

"Who bought it?" she asked.

"Remember that old couple you met in the gallery last week?"

"All wet, with umbrellas?"

"They're called Mr and Mrs Broadway. They live locally – across the river. Great admirers of your mother's work – and the lady comes from an artistic family. She wants me to go round sometime and have a look at some old family water-colours."

"Does she want you to buy them?"

"What? Family ones? Shouldn't think so." He smiled. "I suspect just to tell her they're good and worth such a lot – so that she can say that of course she'd never sell them."

Mum said, "You needn't mock. They might be wonderful."

"They might indeed. So I offered to deliver your painting and take a look."

Mum got up and began gathering things together: car keys, handbag, Kleenex. "I'd better go. I'll be late." She taught art at a school in Culverton three days a week. "Bye!" She kissed them both and left.

Grace couldn't finish her breakfast. She knew it was because of the bus. Mike must have guessed. He said, "If it's really that bad I expect I could take you in the car." Grace was surprised, and touched. But she said no. She didn't want to be thought different – weedy. And besides, there was Adam. She'd get a chance to talk to him on the way to the bus stop.

He was waiting on the bridge.

Grace told him about seeing Clem that morning, and about the dog, and how she'd realized only half the house was haunted; and as she talked an idea came to her.

Clem wasn't in the churchyard. But she

could be in the newspapers.

"It ought to be in the papers, didn't it?" she said. "I mean, they had papers in those days, and it would have been news, if someone drowned. Only – I don't know where you'd find old newspapers."

"Hemsbury," said Adam. "They have them in the reference library there, on microfilm. My dad looks things up in them, for work."

"So we could find out—?"

"We could go on Saturday," said Adam.

They had reached the bus stop. As the bus came in sight they instinctively stopped talking and drew apart.

The bombardment started again as soon as she appeared: "Morning, Grace Heavens!" "Say grace, everyone!" She kept her head down and endured it. Adam was still her friend, and that was all that mattered.

Only once did she and Adam exchange a brief "Hi!" at school, but Sara noticed. "Our little Grace has got a boyfriend at last," she announced to Lauren and Naomi. Grace blushed and denied it. Those three talked about boys all the time.

She got through the ritual humiliation of the bus journey home by thinking ahead: by a quarter past four all this will be over and I'll be walking up the road with Adam ... by half past four I'll be home...

*   *   *

When she opened the door she found a letter on the mat. It was addressed to Mum and was franked with the china museum's name and logo.

Something about Clem. It must be. It was all she could do to stop herself opening it. She paced around the house, restless, for an hour, until she heard the click of the gate.

Mum came in. She looked tired.

"A letter!" said Grace, handing it to her.

"Oh. Thanks." She put it down on the kitchen table and began filling the kettle.

"It's from the museum," said Grace.

"Well, it's not likely to be urgent, then." But she slit it open. "Make me a coffee, will you, love, while I read it?"

Grace spooned coffee into a mug and peered over Mum's shoulder. "What does it say? Is it from Liz Freeman? Is it about Clem – Clemence?"

"Um..." Mum was frustratingly slow to reply. "Not Clemence. Her father. They've been looking through the parish registers and have found out some more about William Ashley and his wife. He died in 1859 – we knew that... Oh! A year later, in 1860, his widow Ann married John Ford. That's the man on the census."

Grace remembered Clem, frightened, in the dimly-lit hall; the man's voice; the smell of him.

"So he *was* her stepfather," she said.

"*John Ford*," Mum read on, "*was a clerk at the china works. In 1860 he was thirty-eight and had never been married. He was a neighbour of the Ashleys – lived at the other end of the terrace with his mother and sisters – and was actively involved with St Leonard's Church; his name appears several times in the church records. Ann Ashley had two more children after she married him: one in 1861 and another two years later. She died in 1869.*"

"And Clemence?" Grace put the mug of coffee on the table. "Doesn't it say anything about her?"

"Nothing. She just disappears. Liz says they checked the list of burials at St Leonard's for 1861, but she wasn't there. Of course, she might have been buried somewhere else."

Or she might have drowned and been swept away, Grace thought.

Mum was reading on.

"What does it say?"

"They considered the possibility that she could have gone into service as a maid – living in someone else's house. Girls of her age often did. But Liz thinks people like the Ashleys and Fords might have considered service a bit beneath them. She'd have expected Clemence to be still at school – at least part-time."

Grace thought about this. "She'd have

wanted to work in the china factory. To be an artist. Like her dad."

"That's what Liz says – that she could have started work part-time." She handed the letter to Grace. "She was probably away from home for some perfectly ordinary reason that night. I don't suppose anything sinister happened."

But Grace thought she didn't sound convinced.

Upstairs, Grace took out the paint box and the papers – smoothed-out now, but fragile where the creases had been.

No wonder Clem hid them, she thought. John Ford had taken away Brush; she wasn't going to let him have the only things left to her of her father's.

She looked at the pictures: the little sketches Clem had done from life, the careful landscape painting that looked so much like the sort of scene her father chose for his china paintings. Clem must have had ambitions to be an artist too.

She imagined them going out together to sketch and paint: around here, on the hills above the river, where she'd seen her that time, and perhaps further afield as well. Clem, and her father, and Brush. Not her mother. Her mother was at home, cooking and cleaning, having those babies who lay in the churchyard.

And then William Ashley died. And Ann Ashley married again – quite soon.

Grace thought about this, and about how Clem must have felt when her beloved father was buried and her mother married Mr Ford and became pregnant within the year—

"Grace?"

Mum's voice came from outside, on the landing. It sounded odd.

Grace opened the door – and felt at once the atmosphere, the sense of someone there, unseen.

She looked at Mum, and understood. This was why her mother had seemed so unsettled lately. "You can feel it too," she said.

Mum nodded. "I've felt it several times."

As they spoke the air began to clear. Mum visibly relaxed. "It's gone."

Grace asked, "Have you seen them? Clem, and Brush, and Mrs Ford?"

"No. But I guessed you had, even though you said you hadn't. With me, it's just the atmosphere..."

"Charley feels it as well."

"But Mike doesn't. I've asked him. He says I'm imagining things. And perhaps I am. But – you've seen things, haven't you? What have you seen?"

Grace didn't want to talk about it. "Just – things. He was horrible, that man. He beat Clem. I think it's her fear we can feel. And I think it's getting worse because of the flood rising."

Mum bit her lower lip. "I don't know what to do – how to help. You hear of exorcisms..."

"Mum! Mike would have a fit."

"Yes, he would!"

They both started to giggle. Grace knew they were getting hysterical.

"But it's not funny," said Mum, wiping her eyes. "We've got to do something. Seriously. I'm frightened."

"I'm going to Hemsbury on Saturday," said Grace.

Mum looked surprised, and Grace realized that she had never said anything like that to her mother before; it would always have been, "Can I go to Hemsbury?" or "Will you take me?"

"I'm going with Adam," she said, "to the library, to look at old copies of *The Hemsbury Chronicle*. You see, I'm sure Clem drowned, and it happened soon – I mean soon, but in March, 1861. If we find out, perhaps the ghosts will go."

CHAPTER EIGHT

Grace was on edge for the next two days, aware of the atmosphere in the house. She noticed how Charley avoided the hall and landing. He would whisk from kitchen to living-room and spring on to his favourite chair, which happened to be Mike's favourite too, and if Grace wanted him upstairs with her she had to pick him up and carry him and would feel his body stiffen. Even when she stroked him he didn't relax.

Mike joked about neurotic females seeing things that weren't there in a way that Mum said was politically incorrect. Grace pointed out that Charley was male, and Mike said Charley was not neurotic at all, just opportunist and after the best chair. The banter went back and forth, and although it was jokey Grace could feel the tensions underneath.

Mum went out on Wednesday, and after she

came home Grace found estate agents' leaflets on the kitchen table. She was shocked. She hadn't realized how much the haunting was affecting her mother.

"There's no peace here," said Mum.

"But you love your studio."

She sighed. "Yes, I do."

On Thursday she shut herself into it, and began a new painting: flowers in a glass jar on a window-sill – the sort of picture people would buy. Grace saw the house leaflets in the wastepaper basket, and felt relief. This was her home, not Clem's; she wasn't going to be driven out of it.

And then Mike came home with a cheque from Mr and Mrs Broadway; he'd delivered *Home from School*.

"Did you value her family water-colours for her?" asked Mum.

"She didn't want them valued, just admired. She wanted to chat and show me round, that's all. So I dutifully admired them. Actually, they were quite interesting: Victorian. Local scenes."

"Who did them?"

"Someone called Pearce, if I remember rightly. An ancestor. Mrs B. does a bit of painting herself. And she's telling all her friends to go and look at your stuff in the gallery, so you'd better get painting, girl, and stop wittering on about ghosts."

"I am! I've been at work all day!" said Mum, laughing. Cheques always cheered her up.

Friday was the day of the museum trip. They set off in the coach at twelve-thirty: two classes and their teachers, all carrying questionnaires, clipboards, pencil cases, and money to spend in the museum shop afterwards. There was a festive atmosphere, made more so for Grace by the knowledge that she could go straight home afterwards instead of back to school. She sat next to Naomi, with Lauren and Sara in front twisting round and chatting to them; her enemies were at the back and for once showing no interest in her.

They reached the museum and crowded into the entrance hall. Mrs Baynes went to the reception desk and Mrs Driver, her voice straining above the hubbub, began explaining what they would see and how they were expected to behave.

They moved off between the glass cases full of painted china, and Grace stopped by the case where William Ashley's teapot was displayed; but the others were more interested in a huge blue and gold glazed vase, like something out of *Ali Baba and the Forty Thieves*.

"You could get inside that!"

"I'm going to draw it," said Sara.

They were supposed to find things to draw. Grace drew the pink teapot, roughly sketching in William Ashley's rural scene, which was too small to copy.

Later they went out into the yard to see the kilns, and then into the long workshop.

Here, Grace felt a change.

This wasn't like the exhibition gallery. It was real: the place where people had actually worked. It was divided up into sections, each of them stone-floored, cool and damp-smelling, with small dusty windows. The school group surged in and filled all the space, dispelling any atmosphere. Grace detached herself from it. She went to one of the windows and looked out and saw the river, high and close.

There were notices around telling you what everything was. They saw a section full of stacked saggars. Grace read the notice and dutifully wrote on her questionnaire, *The word "saggar" comes from "safeguard"*. There were potter's wheels, one of them in use by a man dressed up in old-fashioned clothes. Two women in Victorian dresses but modern plastic-framed glasses were painting moulded china flowers. Another was rubbing something with a cloth. Grace went closer.

"Do you want to try the burnishing?" The woman handed Grace a decorated plate with a gold rim. The gold was dull, dusty-looking. Grace was shown how to wrap a rag around her finger and dip it first in a dish of water, then in one of fine sand, and rub the gold.

"It makes your finger sore after a bit," the woman said. "Imagine doing that all day, with the smell of paint and turpentine in the air."

And yet it must have been satisfying, Grace felt, to see the gold come up deep and gleaming. "Did young girls do this?" she asked.

"Yes. Girls of your age or a bit older would often start with the burnishing. Then if they had the ability they might move on to the painting room."

Clem would have loved that, thought Grace. Burnishing, painting – dreaming of one day being an artist like her father.

She gave the plate back, and moved on.

There was a high desk at the end of the section, where a man sat with his back to her, writing in a ledger. He wore a black jacket and starched white collar, and for an instant she thought he was one of the dressed-up volunteers – but he wasn't. The buzz of school activity had stopped. Silence enclosed her. In panic she swung round, glimpsed rows of women in long dresses, a girl grinding colours. She was in Clem's time; caught here. And the man...

As if he felt her gaze on him, the man turned round; and she knew, even though she had never seen him before, that this was John Ford.

He was not what she had expected. She'd imagined someone big and rough. But he was of medium height, slim, with a clerkish look about him: a watch chain in his pocket, neat side-whiskers, keen grey eyes.

He looked across at her, and Grace felt that he was seeing Clem, and that Clem had once stood here, defiant, outfacing him. Grace wanted to warn her: Don't. Don't provoke this man.

But John Ford was gone. The sound of forty voices all talking at once returned. There was only the desk, and the ledgers and ink-stand – and nearby, a glass case with a yellowing book lying open within it.

Grace stood trembling. No one else seemed to have noticed what had happened. To cover her confusion, she approached the book and looked at the densely-filled pages. They seemed to be a sort of day by day account of happenings at the works. The copperplate writing was cramped and difficult to read, but she made out the top line: *19th February, 1861: Sarah Hoggett, 2 fingers crushed in bone mill...* She flinched, and read on, skimming dates and names: *Walter Farr fined for bringing in beer... 26th February: Esther Leacock, 14 years, taken on as transferer... Catherine Bailey moved to warehouse... Josiah Wells... Clemence Ashley* – her heart gave a jump – *Clemence Ashley dismissed for insolence.* The date was the fourth of March, 1861.

Grace stared at the words. Dismissed for

insolence. So Clem had gone. She had lost her job. And Grace had no doubt it was her step-father John Ford who had caused her to be sacked.

"But why?" she asked Mum when she got home. "What could she have said?"

"I don't suppose you had to say much in those days to be accused of insolence," said Mum. "People got the sack for the slightest thing."

"But she lived with him. You'd think he'd have wanted her wages."

"He probably wanted her humiliation more. And we don't know what she said – or how publicly she said it. He might not have had much option. I wonder what happened afterwards. Perhaps he sent her back to school full-time."

"She'd have hated that. She wanted to be an artist."

But perhaps it had been worth it, to say whatever she'd said to John Ford.

The fourth of March. Only a month before the census – and during that month, Grace thought, Clem had drowned.

CHAPTER NINE

On Saturday morning Adam and Grace caught
the Number 75 bus to Hemsbury. It took them
on a tour of the countryside, stopping at vil-
lages that Grace, who usually travelled by car,
hadn't known existed.

"Look at the flood," said Adam.

From their high position on the road they
could see the plain spread out below, a gleaming swathe of water, steely-coloured in the
early morning light. The river had overflowed
and what had been fields had become a landscape of lakes and islands.

Grace felt quietly excited: about what they
might find out, but also about the floods, the
day out, being with Adam. She had a notebook
and pen in her coat pocket and a five pound
note that Mum had given her for food and
emergencies.

"What sort of emergencies?" Adam asked.

"Chocolate? Crisps?" She giggled.

He clutched his throat. "Aagh! I need chocolate. This is an emergency!"

When they reached Hemsbury Adam took charge. He led the way up the hill to the library and into the reference section.

"I've been here with my dad," he explained.

He found a librarian and asked about back numbers of *The Hemsbury Chronicle*.

"1861?" the woman said. "It'll be on microfilm." She found them a monitor, and they began winding through the papers for March, 1861.

The paper came out on Fridays. The print was dense and small and set in columns, and the articles were boring: political stuff, farming news, trials for uninteresting crimes like theft. There was a mention of floods affecting road travel in the county but nothing dramatic. They reached the Agriculture and Trade section and Adam wound through fast, stopping at the next week's paper.

"Let me have a go," said Grace. They changed places. The image was dark and wobbly, but yes – there was more about the floods. The level of the river was unusually high for the time of year ... a boat capsized at Brentbridge ... roads closed... She moved on to the following week. Still no drownings.

Adam took over again. They were both getting bored. He began skimming faster.

"Wait!" said Grace. She grabbed his arm. "Wind it back."

A man reading at a table nearby glanced up and she went on in a whisper, "I thought I saw her name."

They found the start of the paragraph. The river had overflowed its banks at Hazeley ... some flooding of the china factory premises. Considerable efforts were being made to salvage stock... A lamentable accident – Adam stopped the page there. Clemence Ashley, aged thirteen years, missing since Sunday, was feared to have been swept away and drowned, her shawl having been found entangled in bushes in the flood near Bennet's Mill on the south bank.

"That's it!" said Grace. She felt shock. She realized she hadn't wanted it to be true.

Adam wound the roller on. "There's nothing about how it happened. You'd think they'd say more."

It would be different nowadays, Grace thought. There would be headlines, interviews with distraught parents, TV cameras lingering on the branches where the shawl was caught. And everyone would care.

"What's the date on the paper?"

"Friday the fifteenth of March."

"So she'd been missing since –" she counted backwards – "the tenth."

What happened between the fourth, when

Clem was sacked, and the tenth? Could she have killed herself? But surely no one killed themselves because they lost their job? Not children, anyway.

"Write it down," said Adam. "Everything it says."

Grace scribbled quickly in her notebook.

Adam began winding on. "They might have found the body."

They searched through the whole of March and half of April. There were two other drownings: a drunken man at Hemsbury, a suicide at Brentbridge. But no mention of finding a girl's body.

"So she wasn't found."

"Or she was, but they didn't report it."

That was possible, Grace realized.

But perhaps she wasn't found. Perhaps she didn't go round and round in the pool at Hazeley but escaped into the current and was washed up far away where she'd never be known.

"Where's Bennet's Mill?" she asked.

"No idea."

"Let's ask."

To her surprise she found herself leading the way. The librarian showed them the maps of the Hazeley area. They leaned over the 1850s one, finding, with pleasure, the little shaded rectangles that marked the position of their own homes, and then moving out along the south bank, the side where Adam lived.

"Here!" said Grace.

It wasn't far – perhaps two miles from the footbridge: a collection of shaded boxes and BENNET'S MILL in cramped, old-fashioned print. On the modern map some of the buildings had gone but the name was still there.

"We could find it," said Grace. She was usually a tagging-along sort of person, but now she said decisively, "We could go tomorrow. Will you come with me?"

"Yes!" said Adam – as enthusiastic as she was.

They left the library and walked down to the riverside. They felt excited about their discoveries, full of pent-up energy. Grace had heard that morning on local radio that the river had burst its banks at Hemsbury, and they wanted to see the flood.

The carpark and the municipal gardens were under water. Cast iron seats had become islands with ducks swimming around them. Grace and Adam tried to wade through, but the water was too deep. Adam balanced along a wall, inches above the water. Grace hesitated.

"Come on!" he said. "It's OK."

She followed him, wobbling. Just looking at the water made her feel she'd fall in. Adam came to a gap, leapt, and missed. He emerged with both shoes full of water.

"You did that on purpose!"

"No, I didn't!"

He sat wringing out his socks and laughing.

Sitting on the bus on the way home, Grace felt more subdued. She remembered her vision of Clem, throwing a stick for the dog, in the meadow above the china works. Clem had been wearing a shawl that day: a thick woollen one, black and brown check, with fringing. Grace looked out at the rain and saw in her imagination the same shawl, torn and snagged, caught on bushes above the flood while the current tugged it.

March the tenth.

Today was the second. She counted on her fingers: Sunday week. "It's a Sunday again," she told Adam. "The tenth is a Sunday, like it was the year Clem died."

CHAPTER TEN

The bus dropped them at Hazeley, and Adam went back with Grace to her house. Mum was there, sewing curtains, but Grace was relieved to hear that Mike was at the gallery.

They both explained eagerly what they had found out. Mum fetched an Ordnance Survey map and they showed her Bennet's Mill.

"I think we were meant to find Clem in the newspaper," said Grace. "It's like the book in the museum, open at just the right page—"

"Oh! I phoned Liz Freeman," said Mum, "and told her about that. She was quite apologetic – said she must have passed that book hundreds of times but that you never see what's staring you in the face."

"Did you tell her we were being haunted?"

"No." She frowned. "But I believe we are. And I wish I knew why."

"It might be because the body wasn't

found," said Adam.

Grace didn't like that idea. If Clem was never found, perhaps she would always be here; never leave them alone.

Mum picked up her sewing again. Grace and Adam went upstairs. "Do you want to play a game?" she asked. "I've got Trivial Pursuit, or Monopoly." She wanted a break from thinking about Clem.

"Monopoly," said Adam.

"It'll take ages," she said, pleased.

"That's OK."

They played until evening, then left the board set up. Adam stayed to tea, and afterwards they watched a mindless but funny sitcom with Mike, and then went back to Grace's room, where they found Charley asleep on the Monopoly board, surrounded by scattered houses and hotels.

"You should go to jail, you bad cat," said Grace, cuddling him.

Adam packed away the pieces. "I like this house," he said. "It's peaceful."

"Your voice is quieter here."

"Because yours is. You can't hear yourself think in our house. No one else does think. They just charge about and shout. I bet if we had a ghost no one would even notice."

After he had gone, Grace went back to her room. She thought she might see Clem, but nothing happened. Only later, crossing the landing on the way to the bathroom, did she feel the familiar tension building in the air, like the feeling before a thunderstorm, and knew that if they had found Clem's death it had not changed anything in the house.

What does she want, Grace thought? What can I do? I can't make it not have happened.

She woke next morning to the roar of rain.

All through breakfast they heard it splashing from an overflowing gutter and drumming on the shed roof.

"Looks like a day for the Sunday papers," said Mike.

Grace began putting on wellingtons and an anorak.

"You're not going out in this?" Mum exclaimed.

"I said I'd meet Adam."

She hoped her mother would think she was visiting Adam's house, but Mum guessed. "That place is miles away. You'll get drenched. And it's not safe, going along the riverbank in this. Look at it!"

Grace looked. The rain was coming down like steel rods, hitting the ground and bouncing up. The sky had no break in it.

"The forecast is more of the same," said Mum. "You can't go there today."

"But tomorrow's school. And there won't be time afterwards. I have to go!"

She felt desperate.

Mike got angry. "You're not going, and that's an end of it!"

"You can't stop me!"

Mum picked up her car keys. "I'll take you there."

"For Christ's sake, Jane!" said Mike.

They glared at each other.

"I'm going on my own!" Grace shouted. She felt furious. Why did they have to interfere?

"Phone Adam," said Mum. "Tell him we'll pick him up."

Grace stomped out to the hall. She didn't want Mum to take them. Damn Mike. Damn parents. It was nothing to do with them.

She heard them arguing as she spoke to Adam on the phone. She wondered if he could hear the emotion in her voice, but he merely seemed relieved at the prospect of a lift.

It's not the same for him, she realized; he's never seen Clem; he's not involved, just interested.

Back in the kitchen, the row seemed to have subsided. Mike was washing up. His back expressed disapproval.

"Come on," said Mum.

Outside, she added, "Don't get cross with Mike. He's just worried about you – and me. All this ghost stuff. He thinks I'm encouraging you."

"I hate it when you argue."

"We'll make it up."

They met Adam and Sasha halfway up the road.

"Sasha wanted a walk," Adam said. "Can she come too?"

Grace saw her mother trying not to notice Sasha's soaked fur and muddy paws. "Yes, of course," she said valiantly.

The drive took less than ten minutes, and in that time Sasha had muddied the entire back seat. The road to the old mill was narrow but laid with tarmac. Off to the left were two cottages with landscaped gardens and cars parked outside. The road turned towards the houses, leaving a dirt track that led to the ruined mill. They bumped along it until Mum said, "I'm not going any further – too much mud."

The rain was coming down harder than ever, but Grace and Adam both got out, followed by Sasha, and made a dash for the ruins. After a moment's hesitation, Mum came after them.

"Not much here," said Adam.

Fields sloped down to the river bank. The only feature was the ruined mill, and that was unimpressive: tumbled bricks, mostly buried under the weight of ivy; no roof; a broken wall. The river, only inches below the footpath, was fast, swollen, pocked with rain. Grace looked at the broken branches at its edge and remembered the shawl. She tried to connect this place with her dream. This was where Clem had drowned, struggling in the current, her skirts tangling around her legs.

I ought to see her here, if anywhere, she thought.

Mum stood with her arms folded against the cold, the rain flattening her hair. Adam slipped and scrambled about on the footpath, and Sasha followed him, rooting amongst stones and branches.

"She might find bones," said Adam.

"Not here," Grace said.

But there must be bones, somewhere, she thought. No one can vanish without trace.

The rain beat down, soaking her. She could feel water trickling down the back of her neck and dripping from the hem of her coat into her boots.

"I'm going back to the car," Mum shouted over the sound of the rain.

"And me," said Adam. He whistled up Sasha.

Grace looked around. Rain. Mud. The river rushing by, fast and full.

She'd expected something more – some sign. But there was nothing.

The river rose relentlessly throughout the next week, and although Grace saw no more ghosts, the vision of Clem's shawl, snagged on bushes below the mill, stayed in her imagination.

The bus was still a torment, and she didn't know what to do. Usually she turned away, refused to react. But on Thursday, when Emma snatched the book she was reading and tossed it across the aisle, she felt a surge of fury. She stood up. "Give it back!" she shouted.

"O-oh!" Emma pretended to be scared. Her cronies laughed. The book was passed around. Zoe repeated in a mocking squeak, "Give it back!"

Grace was trembling. She could see Adam, near the back, looking as if he was about to intervene.

Don't, she willed him; please don't.

She sat down, gazed out of the window, feigning indifference. The book would find its way back when they tired of their stupid game.

"Is she crying?" someone crowed.

Grace turned round to show that she was not. She never cried, but she knew she was defeated again.

At home both she and Mum felt the undercurrent of fear and anger in the house. Charley stayed safe in the living-room, and when he had to cross the hall to reach it the fur rose on his back.

It's winding tight, tight, like a spring, thought Grace. It can't go on. Something will break.

CHAPTER ELEVEN

On Friday, when Adam met Grace at the bus stop, he was full of excitement about the floods.

"We're cut off!" he exclaimed. "I had to go out the back way and climb over the fence into the garden of The Black Swan to get on to the road."

"Is your road flooded?"

"Yes! There's a lake by the footbridge now, about –" he demonstrated with his hands and she knew he was exaggerating – "about four feet deep! The path to the craft centre's cut off, and the water's still rising. You'll have to come over at the weekend and see."

"I want to go back to Bennet's Mill on Sunday," said Grace.

"The day she drowned?"

"Yes."

"We might not be able to get along the

footpath by then."

She felt warmed by his use of *we*. "She must have walked along it. And it'll be the same, I'm sure; the same as that day."

"It'll be fun to try, anyway," he said.

The bus came into view.

Grace made a sudden decision. She hung back, let Adam board first, then followed close behind.

No one had ever told her where to sit on the bus, but somehow everyone knew his or her place. Adam always sat with the older boys at the back, Grace near the front – next to the chewing-gum girl, who was called Leanne and who showed her neither interest nor hostility. It had seemed safest not to vary her routine.

But today she felt she could make things change. Adam was going to Bennet's Mill with her; he was her friend and she didn't care who knew it.

Her heart was beating fast, but she tried to look casual as she walked past the empty seat next to Leanne and the staring ranks of girls in the centre, stepped over Zoe's school bag, squeezed past two boys who were fighting, and sat down next to Adam.

The girls looked round, turned and whispered together. A boy whistled. Another one called out, "Hey, Colesey, someone fancies you at last!" Somebody chucked a book at Adam and he turned round and threw it back.

"Settle down, everybody!" called the driver. The bus started up.

Three boys on the back row behind Adam seemed to be his friends.

"Who's she, then?" asked a little dark one with a knowing face.

Before Adam could reply the ginger one said, "Grace! Your name's Grace, isn't it?"

"She's our neighbour," said Adam. "Just moved here."

He made it sound as if he was merely being kind to her, Grace thought. She felt embarrassed, especially when the dark one began to sing, "'Neighbours! Everybody needs good neighbours!" and the back row joined in and Adam turned round and started a mock fight. Had she just made things worse, for him as well as herself?

At the next stop the boy who usually sat next to Adam got on, to a chorus of banter: "She's taken your place, Brycey!" "Move up, you two! Let Brycey on!" But the boy seemed happy to sit on the crowded back row, and after a while they all simmered down and were friendly enough, and the ginger one said, "Here, Grace, you get any more trouble from Big Emma, you let us know. OK?"

For a while Grace and Adam were left alone to talk, and Adam, who looked a bit pink, asked, "Why did you do that?"

She shrugged, trying to look more confident

than she felt. "You're my friend, aren't you?"

"Yes. Sure. Look, Grace, I'd have thumped that Emma for you, but I thought…"

"It's OK. I didn't want you to."

"They'll get fed up in the end," he said. "Start on someone else."

Grace wished she could believe it.

There was a commotion a few rows down.

"Hey, Grace! Grace Heavens! Is he your boyfriend?"

Emma, snorting with laughter, stood swaying with the jolting motion of the bus. Bursts of stifled giggles greeted her as she sat down.

"Morons," Adam commented quietly. And the ginger boy, Craig, shouted, "Shut your fat face, Emma!"

When the bus arrived at Purley Manor the girls moved off first, with backward glances at their victim.

"See you," said Adam. "I'll save a place on the way home, shall I?"

"If you want to." Surely he didn't?

"Well, it livens things up." And he laughed, making her laugh too.

Hurrying inside, she scarcely cared that they were still harassing her. It had been an ordeal, but it wasn't like yesterday. It wasn't a defeat.

On Saturday morning Grace went on to the footbridge to look at the swollen river. Between the boards under her feet she saw the water startlingly close – swift and foam-flecked.

The flood on the far side was impressive. She climbed down the steps until she reached the water level. She saw it lapping at the doorstep of The Black Swan and forming a spreading lake. The Coles' house was safe on its slight rise, but their car-parking space had gone.

Adam came out and waved. "Go round to the craft centre," he shouted. "I'll meet you there."

Grace returned to the north bank and walked half a mile up the road, across the road bridge, and back round to the craft centre. She went to Kathryn Cole's workshop.

Inside, Imogen was arranging jewellery in a glass case. And behind her Adam and his mother were trying to fix a large blue wall-hanging with planets and stars on it to the back wall of the shop, balancing on precarious-looking bits of furniture and arguing with each other in loud voices.

Kathryn called out, "Hi, Grace! Nice to meet you. I'm Kathy. Come and have a look round."

Grace went in. The ceiling was hung with mobiles and wind chimes, and there were dream-catchers in every size from penny to dinner-plate.

Imogen saw Grace's fascination with the dream-catchers.

"I can make those," she said. "Shall I show you? Mum, can I get your box of odd bits?"

"Yes," said Kathy – then screeched, "Adam!" as her son leapt from a high stool to a rickety table which wobbled under his weight. "If you're going to mess about, you can go," she said.

Grace caught his eye and they exchanged smiles.

"Adam's showing off because you're here," Imogen confided. "He likes you a lot."

Grace felt herself blushing. She rummaged busily in the box, which was full of coloured yarn, beads, brass rings and sequins. "This is great!" she said.

The girls settled down on the floor at the back of the workshop, and Imogen started Grace off with a ring and showed her how to weave the web. Soon Grace had a small blue dream-catcher with green and purple beads and a jay's feather hanging from it. She put it in her pocket when they went out with Adam to look at the flood.

At midday Kathy closed the shop for an hour and drove them back to her house for lunch with the rest of the family. Afterwards they watched a video and played Scrabble; and all the time Grace felt she was in limbo, waiting, thinking about tomorrow, the tenth of March – the day Clem had drowned.

As Grace was leaving, Adam asked, "What

time are you going to Bennet's Mill?"

"Ten?"

"I'll meet you on the road bridge."

Grace woke early; and at once her mind was active. She imagined Clem waking, today, in 1861. How would she have been feeling? She had lost her job – the link with her father – and been sent back to school. Brush was banished to the yard. Clem must have been full of anger against John Ford, that keen church-goer – who would surely be worshipping at St Leonard's this morning with his wife.

No doubt he expected Clem to go too. But Clem wouldn't want to – her choice had been to spend Sundays out sketching with her father and Brush. Perhaps she defied her step-father. Perhaps on that Sunday, when she was so angry and hurt, she got up early and went out before they were awake, knowing that she'd be beaten for it but not caring.

And there, in the bedroom, Grace saw her.

She was by the wash-stand, putting on her bonnet; the brown and black checked shawl was around her shoulders.

She stepped to the door, paused to listen as she opened it, then slipped outside.

Grace was on her feet.

"Clem!" she cried out. "Don't go!"

The thought came that she could stop her, prevent what must happen. She ran out on to the landing and followed the girl downstairs into the hall, which was changed again to its dark Victorian existence, lit only by a fanlight over the door. The figure seemed to blend with the shadows.

Oh, come back! Please come back! thought Grace.

But she heard a door open; there was a gust of cold air from the place where the kitchen should have been, a flicker of movement – and Clem was gone. Grace was alone in the light, unhaunted hall.

The weather was cold – as it had been the day Clem Ashley went out and never returned.

Grace zipped up her jacket and shoved her hands in her pockets as she ran up the road, past the china factory, to the bridge. It was five to ten. She waited there, looking out towards Bennet's Mill, seeing the frost-whitened fields, the bare trees with their hint of green, thinking of Clem walking the lanes with Brush.

She saw Adam first – and then, behind him, to her disbelief and anger, Luke, Josh and the dog.

Adam separated himself from the others and came towards her.

"Sorry, Grace," he said.

CHAPTER TWELVE

"Mum and Dad have gone to a craft fair at Ludlow – they arranged it ages ago. Imogen's gone with them. And I'd promised to mind the little ones. I just forgot all about it."

Grace was distraught. "We can't have them tagging along!"

She walked away, forcing him to follow.

"It's OK," he said. "I'm not supposed to take them near the water anyway, so we won't come with you—"

She swung round on him. "But you said you would!"

"Grace, I promised Mum."

"You promised me!"

She knew she was being unfair, but she couldn't help herself. She wanted him to come with her. She was afraid of what she might encounter at Bennet's Mill, and she wanted him there.

"I saw her," she said. "Just now. Going out." Her voice shook. "I couldn't stop her."

"Grace –" he half turned, watching Luke and Josh, who were running up and down the pavement with Sasha – "I do want to come. Honestly."

Luke approached them, struggling to restrain Sasha. "Can we go and look at the floods?"

Adam took the dog's lead from him. "You know we can't go near the river with Josh."

"Josh'll be all right," said Luke. He ran and grabbed his brother by his anorak hood. "I'll hold on to him."

A noisy struggle ensued.

Grace said, "I'll go on my own, then."

She turned away, knowing Adam would follow.

"No, wait!" He ran round in front of her. "I could bring them."

"But you're not allowed to."

"It'll be all right. It will. I want to come."

He began rounding up the boys, lecturing them: "We're going for a walk along the river bank. It's quite a long way—"

"To see the floods?" asked Luke, capering.

"Floods!" echoed Josh.

"If you don't behave, we'll turn back. Are you going to be good?"

"Yes!" said Luke. He looked solemn.

"I'm good! I'm good!" sang Josh. "Sasha's good, too."

"Let's go, then."

Grace felt angry and guilty and contrite all at once. It wasn't Adam's fault, but she didn't want Luke and Josh there. They could spoil everything; Clem might not appear. She said, "Adam, don't bring them. You'll only get into trouble."

But it was too late. They were on their way.

Grace knew the day had already gone wrong. She should not have manoeuvred Adam into disobeying his mother. But she'd been desperate. Clem was gone, vanished on her last walk, and Grace wanted to hurry after her, to be there, to do – she didn't know what, only that she was bound up with Clem and had to follow.

Adam was aware of how she felt, but Josh and Luke capered about, exclaiming over flooded gardens and mud and debris, and squealing with excitement when water lapped over the edge of the path.

Most of the way they walked along the higher footpath. The lower one that the fishermen used was under water. Soon they drew opposite the place where Grace and Adam had climbed out on to the mound of tiles. It was the last familiar landmark. After that the river curved and ran between steep banks, hung with trees. The path was uneven and slippery, and the water only inches below it. Grace began to wonder if they would reach Bennet's Mill, or if the path would be flooded even at this higher level.

"Hold on to Luke," said Adam. "I'll take Josh."

Grace took Luke's hand, and Luke chatted about monsters; he'd seen a film on television about Loch Ness. Soon he tried to wriggle his hand free of hers, but Grace held on. "Stay close," she said. "It's steep here."

"I'm not frightened."

"Are you tired yet? It's a long way." She gazed ahead at the unfamiliar stretch of river bank. Surely Bennet's Mill must be near, now? Adam was in front of her with Josh, the dog scampering between the two groups, occasionally splashing in at the river's edge and leaping out in a flurry of drops.

"I'm never tired," said Luke. "Look at Sasha, being silly!" She felt the eagerness in his hand; he wanted to catch Sasha up and be silly with her.

Then Adam called out, "Grace!" and pointed, and she looked ahead, and saw the ruined mill around the next bend.

And she saw something else. Between her and Adam, only a few yards away, stood two people: Clem Ashley and John Ford.

Grace stopped, and drew in her breath.

There was no sound, but she saw that they were arguing. The man seized Clem by the shoulders and shook her, while the dog, Brush, opened and shut his mouth in a frenzy of silent barking.

Grace felt the air around her grow intensely cold. She tried to call Adam, but her voice would not come. Luke's hand slipped from hers.

The soundless quarrel became more violent. Clem was shouting and tears ran down her face. The man grabbed her by the arm and propelled her in the direction of home. She reached back, to Brush, who jumped up at John Ford's leg. Grace saw the man's face for an instant: fury and frustration flashed across it. He reached down, seized the dog, and hurled it into the river.

Grace found her voice. "No!" she screamed. "Brush! Brush!"

He was struggling; he would drown.

Without further thought she leapt after him and plunged into the water. The current caught her and she was swept away from the bank. She felt her long skirts – or was it weeds? – catching around her legs and saw the brown speck that was Brush being whirled away.

From the bank came sounds of shouting. She surfaced, gasped, saw trees, branches, whipping past.

It's my dream, she thought. It was me, as well as her. We're both going to drown.

And then she was swept up hard against a

tangle of branches: caught in a half-submerged tree; struck in the face and neck by sharp twigs. She caught hold, held on, while the current tore at her.

She heard a shout. She turned, spitting out water, and saw Adam, on the bank. He was holding on to a tree and trying to reach her with a long branch. It was within reach of her hand.

"Grab it! Quick! I'll pull!"

But she daren't let go; the current would take her, instantly.

"Grace!"

"I can't!"

"Just do it!"

He sounded so fierce that she had to obey. She reached for the branch with one hand, then, with a gasp of fear, the other. She screamed as she felt herself sink. But Adam hauled on the branch; she kicked out across the pull of the flood; felt the bank slippery under her weight; the branch fell away and Adam let go of the tree and grabbed her upper arms. At once she began slipping. She thought: he can't hold me! For a terrifying moment it seemed that her waterlogged clothes would pull her back and take him with her, but he held on; and slowly they both crawled out and up the bank.

They crouched there, on hands and knees, gasping with shock and cold. Then Adam stood up and turned on her: "You idiot! You bloody idiot! Why did you do that? I told you he was OK. I'd got him. He was safe. Why—"

"I–had to–he–he–swept away," Grace gasped incoherently. She saw that Josh was there, wet through like Adam. Why? she wondered. Sasha was shaking muddy drops. Luke, the only one still dry, stood white and shocked. And an elderly man who looked vaguely familiar was picking his way cautiously along the river bank towards them.

Adam persisted, "For God's sake, Grace, you nearly drowned!"

And then Luke began to cry, and so did Grace. She wiped her eyes, and found that there was blood on her; the cuts sustained in her collision with the tree began to sting. The elderly man reached Luke and Josh and took hold of their hands. He said to Adam, "Are you all right? Are they all safe? You've had a lucky escape. Better bring everyone back to the house to get dry."

The house was one of the cottages that Grace had seen before, set back from the ruins of Bennet's Mill.

She entered, still shaking, but aware that Adam had put his arm around her shoulders. Conscious of this, she noticed almost nothing else until she saw, straight ahead of her on the wall above the settee, Mum's painting, *Home*

113

from School. And then she knew why the old man, and also his wife, who had just come in, looked familiar.

"You're the ones who bought the painting," she said through chattering teeth.

They both looked at her, surprised. And then the woman exclaimed, "It's Grace, isn't it? I remember you, in the gallery. Oh dear, this is such a shock. We must get you all dry. And we'd better phone your parents. I've brought down blankets and towels..."

Grace remembered their name then: Broadway.

Mrs Broadway said to her husband, "You take the boys up to the bathroom. Grace can use the kitchen. Come along, dear. Don't get upset. We must get you dry, and clean up those cuts on your face – that's all. There's no harm done."

But there is, there is, thought Grace. I'm safe, but Clem is dead. She was swept away and drowned because of Brush and no one could save her, not even me.

And she began to shake and cry as she stripped off her wet clothes and dropped them on the tiled floor and dried herself on the towel.

She emerged smelling of antiseptic and wrapped in a turquoise candlewick dressing-gown and fluffy slippers a size too large. Adam, who had just come downstairs wearing

Mr Broadway's dressing-gown, burst out laughing, and Grace laughed too, and then, to her own surprise, began to cry again in great heaving sobs.

Adam looked alarmed, and Mrs Broadway said, "Grace needs a cup of tea, for the shock. I think we all do." And she went to put the kettle on.

"Sit down here near the fire," said Mr Broadway.

Grace sat in a squashy armchair, opposite Adam. She let the slippers drop to the floor and tucked her feet under her.

The little boys were unusually subdued. Luke knelt on the hearth rug, drying Sasha with a towel. Josh, with his thumb in his mouth, ran to Adam and curled up on his lap.

Grace tried to speak, and found that her voice shook and was out of control. "What ... what happened?"

"Didn't you see?" asked Adam. "Luke threw a stick for Sasha and it went in the river—"

"I didn't mean it to," said Luke. His lip trembled.

"But it did," said Adam, "and Sasha went in, and I was scared for her and let go of Josh and ran forward and shouted. You shouted something, too, and then – I don't know how – Josh slipped and fell in. I got to him straight away – just grabbed him and pulled him out –

but he was soaked, and then Sasha came out with the stick, and I called out, "It's OK! I've got him!" and then – I couldn't believe it – I saw you in the water, right out there, being swept away!"

"So I ran," said Luke.

"Yes, Luke ran to the house, and I waded in, and held on to the bushes, but you were swept past. It was lucky you got caught on that tree or I'd never have reached you."

Grace stared at him, aghast. She could have drowned Adam, too.

Luke was anxious to be appreciated. "I ran very fast, and shouted," he said.

"You did well," said Mrs Broadway.

Adam turned to Grace. "But why did you go in? Was it Sasha?"

"No. I never saw Sasha. I saw Brush. I saw what happened."

They exchanged a glance and fell silent. The Broadways looked puzzled for a moment, but then Grace began to shake visibly again, and Mr Broadway looked at his wife and said, "Where's that tea, Clem?"

CHAPTER THIRTEEN

For an instant Grace thought: It's her! It's Clem! And then common sense told her that was impossible; it was over a century ago that Clem Ashley had been swept away. But why did Mrs Broadway have Clem's name, here, in this house, so near to the place where Clem had died?

She jumped up and followed her into the kitchen.

"No, you sit down, dear," the woman began, but Grace said urgently, "He called you Clem. Is that your name? Clem?"

"Yes." She looked surprised. "It's short for Clemence. Quite an unusual name. I don't suppose you've heard it before."

She put cups and a sugar bowl on a tray. "Here, you take this cup. Put a couple of biscuits in your saucer – go on, take another one. That's right. Yes, it's a family name."

She followed with the tea things and settled down with what seemed to Grace agonizing slowness. "My mother was called Clemence," she said, "and so was my great-grandmother. In fact, it was my great-grandmother who painted the water-colours your father came to see."

"She painted? Clemence?" Grace felt a mounting excitement.

"Yes. Do you want to see?" Mrs Broadway seemed glad to have taken Grace's mind off her earlier distress. "They're in the dining-room."

She led Grace into a room full of polished dark wood and damask curtains. There were four paintings. The first two, placed together, were quite small, but full of fine detail, reminding Grace of William Ashley's landscapes. One was of Brentbridge, looking strangely traffic-free and rural, but recognizable by its clock tower. The other was of Hazeley, with the footbridge, the wharves, the brown-sailed barges, the bare hills beyond. Grace remembered her glimpse of that scene in Clem's day. It was the same.

"See, here is her signature: *C. Pearce* – " Mrs Broadway was obviously proud of the paintings – "and the date, *1874.*"

1874. Clem Ashley would have been about twenty-five then, had she lived. But who was Clemence Pearce?

Mrs Broadway took her across the room to

an alcove. The painting there was larger, and dated 1878. "Your father thought this one was the best." It was a rural scene – trees, cottages, a winding road. "I believe it's a village near Brentbridge. She lived in that area most of her life..."

But Grace wasn't listening. She was staring at the last painting. It was smaller, and made Grace think at once of the tiny pictures Clem Ashley had drawn as a child. There was a meadow, and a line of trees, and behind them a church spire. But in the centre were two figures: a girl in bonnet and shawl throwing a stick, and a little dog, a bright-eyed terrier, leaping to retrieve it.

Grace was bewildered. "It's her!" she said. "It's Clem!" But she didn't understand. She peered at the date: 1876. Who was this Clemence Pearce? How did she know?

Mrs Broadway, misunderstanding, said, "Yes, I've often thought it could be a self-portrait. Or perhaps it's her daughter."

Grace was trying to work things out. Married women didn't keep their names. "Was she *Mrs* Pearce?" she asked.

"Oh, yes. Her daughter, my grandmother, was Miss Ann Pearce, and she married William Rainer, so my mother was Clemence Rainer..."

Grace shook this information aside, brought her back to the great-grandmother.

"What was Clemence Pearce's name before she married?"

"Now that I can't tell you. And even if I could it wouldn't mean much. You see, she was brought up by an aunt who was married and lived at Brentbridge, and she took the aunt's surname. There's a story in the family that she ran away from home – she'd have been twelve or thirteen then; must have been quite a handful, by all accounts – and even –" she hesitated, with an anxious glance at Grace – "even that she nearly drowned in the attempt—"

"Nearly drowned?" Grace began to tremble.

"Yes. Perhaps I shouldn't have—"

But Grace interrupted breathlessly: "So someone rescued her? She didn't drown? She escaped? She grew up?"

"Well, yes." She smiled. "Obviously she grew up, or I wouldn't be here… But why—?"

Grace couldn't wait. She darted away, burst into the living-room, and exclaimed, "Adam! Adam! Clem didn't drown! She escaped, and went to Brentbridge, and got married, and Mrs Broadway is her great-granddaughter!"

"Do you believe me?"

It felt vital to Grace that the Broadways should not think she was making up ghost stories, that they should understand that this was real.

"I believe you saw these ghosts," said Mrs Broadway carefully, "and I also believe there are more things in heaven and earth than our minds can understand."

"It's very strange," agreed Mr Broadway, and he told them about a ghostly experience he'd had as an airman during the war. "No one can convince me it didn't happen."

Grace was thinking. She remembered the 1850s map, with the mill and the blocks of cottages shaded in. The Broadways' home was old; it would have been here in Clem's time. Someone rescued Clem, and brought her ashore, possibly to this same cottage.

But she never went home. The change of name proved that. Perhaps she asked her rescuers not to take her home; or perhaps she told them she came from Brentbridge. Somehow she managed to get to her aunt's – and there she stayed. She never went back to her mother and John Ford.

Grace explained all this, and the others considered it – all except Josh, who had fallen asleep on Adam's lap and looked, Grace thought, surprisingly endearing.

It was Luke who suddenly said, "What about the dog?"

"Brush?" With horror Grace remembered the brown speck being swept rapidly downstream. "Oh, poor Brush! He must have drowned!"

"Not necessarily," said Mr Broadway. "Dogs are rather better than humans in that situation. All the same, I doubt if they found each other again."

Grace thought of Clem and Brush, always together. Clem must have been heartbroken. "She'd have hated John Ford," she said. "I'm not surprised she wouldn't go back."

"I wonder," said Mrs Broadway, "how long it was before Clem's mother knew she hadn't drowned – if she ever did? And whether she wanted her home."

"She didn't deserve her," said Grace.

"Oh! That's hard. It wasn't easy for a wife in those days to defy her husband."

"She should have been on Clem's side," Grace said.

She felt tears spring to her eyes again, and Mrs Broadway got up and said, "We really ought to ring these children's parents."

The next few days were full. Both Adam and Grace were in trouble with their parents, and Grace had to insist to Mum and Mike that it was not Adam's fault, that she had been to blame. "Tell Kathy," she insisted. Then on Monday their photographs were in the local paper with the headline, CHILDREN IN RIVER SNATCH DRAMA. There was even an editorial about the dangers of allowing children to play near rivers. A bit different to Clem's day, thought Grace, remembering the brief paragraph in *The Hemsbury Chronicle*.

She still had trouble on the school bus – if anything it got worse for a while – but she sensed an undertone of admiration. Not only was her photograph in the paper but she had a boyfriend and he'd rescued her from drowning – dead romantic, as Naomi said.

Mrs Broadway was in the paper, too, smiling beside a William Ashley vase at the museum. There was no mention of a ghost – they had all agreed to keep quiet about that – but there were enough clues to link Clemence Pearce with Clemence Ashley, and Mrs Broadway was delighted to find herself a descendant of William Ashley.

Grace came home from school on Thursday to find her mother clearing away tea things. She'd had visitors: Kathy and Mrs Broadway, one after the other.

She handed Grace a small flat parcel. "Mrs Broadway left this for you."

Grace unwrapped it eagerly. Inside was a Clemence Pearce painting: the one of the girl with the little dog. Grace laid it on the table and looked at it and knew that she wanted it very much. "Is it to keep?"

"Yes. She thinks it should hang in this house – to bring Clem Ashley home. She says that when Clem painted it she had a little daughter – a child she had named Ann, after her mother. Mrs Broadway thinks that at that time Clem remembered her own childhood and regretted the rift with her mother. Her mother had died in 1869 and they were probably never reconciled."

And that's what she wanted, Grace realized. Clem wanted to tell her mother what really happened. She wanted to come home, to her rightful place, and forgive, and be forgiven.

"Where will you hang it?"

Grace's first thought was her bedroom. Then she changed her mind. The bedroom wasn't the most haunted place. "Can I hang it in the hall?" she asked.

They found the place at once: a small space that seemed to need a painting. And when it was hung it looked, Grace thought, exactly right, as if the space had been waiting for just this picture and was now complete.

All week the flood had slowly subsided, leaving behind it a tide-line of weed and polythene hanging in the trees. The weather changed, and grew warmer. On Sunday morning Grace said, "The house feels different."

"It's fresh air," said Mike.

And it was true: Mum had gone round opening windows to let in the spring. But it wasn't just ventilation; the whole fabric of the house seemed to have undergone a change: it had a warmer, kinder feel, a sense

of being at peace with itself. Charley felt it.
He had found a patch of sunlight on the hall
table and lay there asleep, his tail curled
around the telephone.

"Let's go for a walk," said Mum.

She and Mike began putting on their out-
door shoes.

"Can we call in at the museum?" asked
Grace.

"If you like. Why?"

Grace ran upstairs, to the corner cupboard
in her bedroom, and brought out William
Ashley's paint box. "It belongs there, with his
work," she said.

When they came out of the museum they
walked along by the river, all the way to the
tile bank and back. The air smelt mild and
sweet. Mum picked stems of pussy willow and
branches with sticky buds just opening.

As they came back up the road Grace heard
barking. She looked up and saw Sasha bound-
ing towards her and Adam running across the
footbridge.

Her parents turned down towards the
house. Grace climbed up the grass bank and
squealed as the dog's weight and muddy paws
landed on her chest.

Adam called out, "I'm walking Sasha – up
the top field."

It was an invitation.

Grace remembered the top field – where she'd seen Clem Ashley throwing a stick for Brush.

But Clem won't be there today, she thought, or ever again; it'll just be me and Adam.

"Grace? Are you coming?" Adam shouted.

"Yes!" She began to run, the dog leaping beside her.